TRANS-HUMAN

—BOOK 3—

DAVID SIMPSON

TRANS-HUMAN

BY DAVID SIMPSON

ACKNOWLEDGMENTS

Thank you to all of my readers for your kind support, reviews, and for telling your friends about my writing.

I want to thank Paul Hurley and Wilhelm Emilsson for their valuable insight.

And, more than anyone, I want to thank my wife, Jennifer. I simply couldn't succeed without her tireless help and support. She's the best wife in the universe and all other universes too.

PROLOGUE

It has been nineteen months since the A.I. turned against humanity and was, subsequently, destroyed. In the meantime, James Keats has turned over the A.I.'s powers to a non-intelligent, easily controlled operating system. He and Thel have left the planet and have spent six months vacationing on Venus, which has been newly terraformed without the consent or knowledge of the Governing Council.

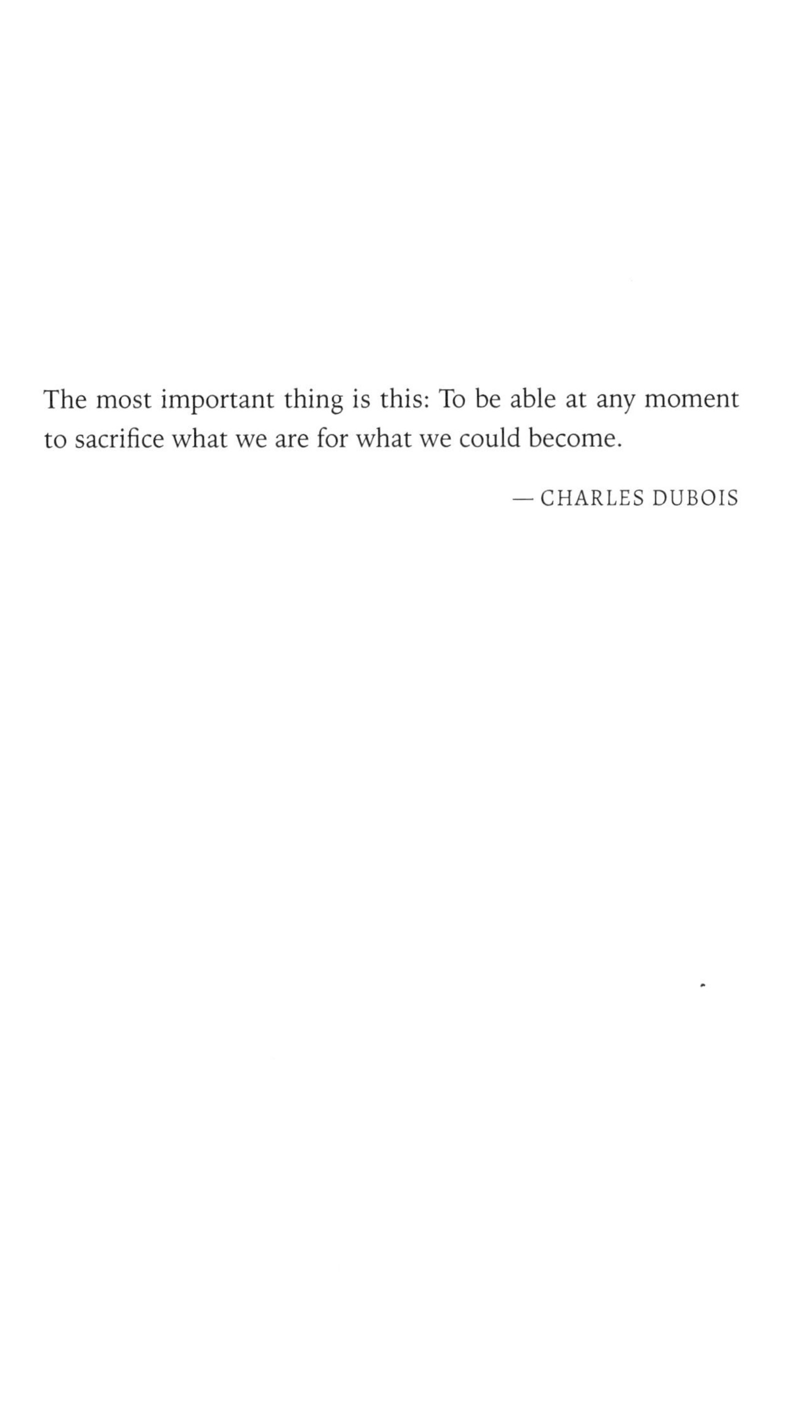

The most important thing is this: To be able at any moment to sacrifice what we are for what we could become.

— CHARLES DUBOIS

PART I

1

WAKING UP had rarely been such a pleasure. Thel opened her eyes to the brilliant Venusian sunshine and smiled. She stepped out of her bed and her toes were greeted by the warm floorboards that had been heated all morning in the sun; the balcony was open, and the white drapes were blowing gently in the morning breeze. The sun lit the emerald mountains, and the lake twinkled calmly. Thel rested her naked body against the warm palm tree that grew at a sixty-degree angle and cut through the balcony floor. Her skin had browned so much in the sun over the last six months that they were nearly the same color, giving them the illusion of being melded together.

She was going to miss the perfection of Venus.

Her mind's eye flashed in her eyes, and she answered when she saw it was James calling. "Hello, Superman."

"Hi there, Supergirl," James replied. "I got the band back together!"

"Almost," Thel pointed out.

"Almost," James conceded. "Djanet is busy at the Council headquarters, but Rich and Old-timer are here with me," he happily informed her.

"I'm not going to like having to put clothes on," Thel said, donning a playful frown.

"Hey, I never said you have to. I'm sure Rich and Old-timer won't mind..."

"Stop right there," Thel cut him off. "I'll throw *something* on. I'm just going to miss the freedom of this place, now that we're letting the cat out of the bag."

"I know what you mean," James replied, as he skimmed across the surface of the Venusian ocean, flanked by Old-timer and Rich. "Listen, we're going to be there soon, but first I want to swing by the falls to show the guys, okay?"

"*Show off* to the guys, you mean," Thel teased. "Okay, flyboy. See you soon," she said before signing off.

James smiled. She was right: He did feel as though he were showing off his new toy. He wasn't sure if it was the right thing to reveal to the world that he had terraformed Venus; he even worried that he might be revealing its existence just so that he could get the chance to revel in his creation for an audience. He would never really be sure of his own motivations. All he knew was that he was happy to be with his friends and to be showing them the new crown jewel of the solar system.

He patched back into communication with Rich and Old-timer. "Thel's really happy to see you guys again."

"It'll be nice to see her too," Old-timer replied. "I have to admit, I can't blame you for keeping this place to yourself for the last six months. It's spectacular."

"You haven't seen anything yet," James grinned. "Follow me!" James blasted forth into supersonic flight.

Old-timer and Rich smiled at each other after their initial astonishment and then followed suit. It had been a long time since they'd seen their former commander and friend and an even longer time since they'd seen him with such childlike enthusiasm. There had been a time, long before the events that had caused James to have to destroy the A.I., when James was always filled to the brim with youthful optimism. The slow collapse of his marriage and the pressure he had been under to terraform Venus had withered that away to nothing, and it seemed as though it might be gone forever. Rich and Old-timer were happy to see it back.

"Holy..." Rich whispered as James's destination became apparent on the horizon. "What the hell is *that*?"

"It's...my God...it is the most phenomenal thing I have ever seen," Old-timer replied.

A massive wall of white vapor stretched from one side of the horizon to the other and stretched up to the blue sky, gleaming and a thousand times the size of the largest mountain on Earth.

"James...what are we looking at?" Old-timer asked.

James's smile beamed as his companions caught up to him and they collectively slowed their approach. "This is my masterpiece," he replied. "You have to see it up close. Come on," he said excitedly as he guided his companions down until they were skimming just above the ocean's waves. The trio flew toward the wall of white and then, just as they were about to enter, James pulled up. "Okay...hold up."

Rich and Old-timer stopped and floated just above the ocean surface.

"What's going on?" Rich asked.

"You're going to love this," James replied. "Deactivate your cocoons and shut down your minds' eyes. I want you to *fully* experience this."

All three men deactivated their magnetic fields and were suddenly overwhelmed by the roar. Rich put his hands up to his ears, while James laughed.

"I've never heard anything like it!" Old-timer yelled above the roar. "Is that what I think it is?"

"It's the biggest waterfall in the known universe!" James yelled back, smiling. "It's a canyon ten times as long and as deep as the Grand Canyon with an ocean spilling over the side! I want to take you over the edge nice and slow. Get ready for the experience of a lifetime!"

He turned and started skimming the waves once again and Rich and Old-timer followed closely behind. Old-timer's stomach jumped as they entered the massive wall of mist generated by the falls, and the edge of the falls emerged like a dream. Rich began to look queasy, and he unconsciously reached out and grabbed James's jacket sleeve; he held on as tight as he could as the trio reached the edge and flew down into the white abyss.

2

"Holy crap!" Rich yelled out as he held on to James's arm for dear life and began to laugh hysterically. "This is amazing!"

James let the mist fill his lungs and clear his mind as he coasted through the beautiful whiteness, until the falls disappeared from sight. The trio flew through the whiteness until they emerged on the opposite side, turning to face the wall of mist and the still-roaring falls. Below them, the water gleamed in the bright sunshine and swirled angrily.

"Isn't it incredible?" James asked.

"I've never seen anything like it," Old-timer nodded, impressed.

"It's...I know I should have an impressive adjective here but all I can think is...wow," Rich added.

James smiled. "There are twelve more just like it on the planet. The mist helps reflect the sun's rays and to keep the air currents flowing properly to cool the planet. The falls themselves generate enormous amounts of energy, which supercharges the planet's ionosphere."

"How is charging the ionosphere productive?" Old-timer asked.

"It's not just productive. It's crucial," James replied. "When I had access to all the information in the A.I.'s mainframe, I searched for information that would be useful for terraforming. I came across an amazing discovery. A scientist who lived in the late nineteenth and early twentieth centuries, Nikola Tesla, had discovered a way to transmit power wirelessly."

Old-timer knitted his brow.

Rich appeared baffled. "I'm not sure I follow you."

"No, you do. It's just like I said," James replied. "As amazing as it sounds, before the twentieth century had even begun, a scientist had learned how to transmit electricity *without* wires. The technology had been hidden from the world after his death because certain governments wanted to maintain their power by forcing the use of fossil fuels, limiting those who could access it and keeping most of the world poor for economic reasons. Eventually, the wireless electricity technology was completely forgotten—but a record of it was still in the A.I.'s database."

"So...are you saying that Venus is...electrified?" Rich asked.

James smiled and nodded. "Yes! Isn't it incredible? Venus takes in much more solar energy than the Earth, and with the additions of these falls all over the planet's oceans, the ionosphere is supercharged and has far more energy than its future inhabitants could ever need. You'll never need a fusion implant on Venus."

"That truly is incredible, Commander," Rich replied. "It's genius."

James laughed, "I never would have been able to do this without the information I had access to when I was operating the A.I. mainframe."

The trio stopped for a moment and let the spectacle of the falls sink in. James watched the power of the water as it churned so far below and couldn't help but think of his former wife. He'd been considering naming one of the falls after her. It was so rare for a person to die these days—the art of commemorating someone's life seemed to have been lost.

"You miss Katherine, don't you?" a warm voice spoke.

James turned to Old-timer and smiled, surprised that his friend could read him so easily. "Yes. Of course I do."

"What?" Old-timer asked, confused.

"I miss Katherine," James said. Old-timer's look of confusion didn't subside. "Didn't you just ask me if I missed Katherine?" James asked.

Old-timer shook his head. "No, I didn't say a word."

"Oh," James smiled, embarrassed, "I guess it was..." He didn't finish his sentence, as he turned to see that Rich had floated several meters away and out of earshot. He was staring up at the white mist as it climbed hundreds of meters into the sky. "That's the damnedest thing," James said.

"What happened?" Old-timer asked.

"I just...I swear someone asked me if I missed Katherine. It was as clear as a bell."

Old-timer could see the sudden distress in his friend's expression. It was only natural that James was having a harder time getting over the death of his former wife than he would admit to himself. It was true that James loved Thel, but he would always be haunted by the death of Katherine at the hands of the A.I. He put his arm on James's shoulder and said, "It's probably just the sound of the falls messing with your ears. Come on, kid. Let's go see that woman of yours. And I could use a replicator right about now. I'm starving!"

James smiled and nodded. "Yes, of course. Let's go." He activated his magnetic field and contacted Rich. "Let's move out, buddy."

In seconds, the trio was blasting up into the sky and away from the waves, heading toward James's Venusian hideaway.

The mystery of the voice haunted him all the way home.

3

Thel stood on the balcony of the third-floor entrance of their beautiful lakeside home and waved the three men inside as they shut down their magnetic fields and landed softly on the lush carpeting. She wore a yellow sundress and was holding a glass jug of cold lemonade. "Hello, men!" she greeted with a smile.

"Hello, woman!" Old-timer responded as he embraced her and then pulled back immediately to take in the changes in her appearance. "You're so golden!" he commented, referring to her tan.

"I've had a nice vacation, as you can see," she replied, continuing to smile. "And your flight suits are all damp from the falls. I can see he took you in for a close look."

"Oh, sorry about that, milady," Old-timer smiled as he stepped back from her. "And while I believe *you* are his pride and joy, my dear, he did take us to the falls. They were spectacular...and spectacularly wet."

"Thel, hi," Rich said as he eyed her drink. "It's nice to see you. Say, that lemonade looks pretty good, and it's awfully hot."

"Hello to you too, Rich," Thel replied. "I promise you can have some of this lemonade once you've dried your clothes. You and the boys can use the dryers in the bathroom." She pointed toward the back of the house.

"Much obliged," Old-timer replied with a small bow as he and Rich withdrew.

James met Thel's eyes, and then stepped to her and kissed her. "I missed you."

"You've only been gone for an hour and a half, and I was sleeping through most of it," Thel replied, kissing him back.

"I stand by my statement of missing."

She laughed and gently pulled herself away from him. "You're all damp too, flyboy. I think you better join the boys in the locker room and dry off."

"Fine," James replied before kissing her once more. "I'd rather be with *you* in the locker room though."

"Tonight," she replied. Thel made him feel as though he were the luckiest man alive.

Old-timer and Rich were already under the air vents as James entered the white-tiled bathroom. "How do you point the vents down? I need to dry my pants," Rich asked Old-timer, who responded by doing it for him with his mind's eye. "Thanks," Rich replied.

"So...what do you guys think of the place?" James asked.

"It's paradise," Old-timer replied. "Are you sure you want to tell everyone about this? I'm sure you could keep it a secret a little longer. Since the Council canceled plans to terraform Venus for the foreseeable future, no one is going to be looking your way."

James smiled. "Are you thinking you and Daniella would like to put up a little villa somewhere?"

"Maybe." Old-timer smiled back.

James laughed. "Well, you're welcome to, but I think the longer I keep it a secret the more upset the Council is going to be with me when they find out about it. Six months is probably bad enough."

Suddenly, James's mind's eye flashed open. It was an emergency call from Aldous Gibson, Chief of the Governing Council.

James sighed. "Speak of the devil."

"What is it?" Old-timer asked.

"Chief Gibson. This should be interesting."

"Wow. I'm not here," Rich said before James answered.

"Keats here."

"Commander Keats..." Gibson began before pausing; he seemed to struggle to finish his sentence, "we have an...extremely serious situation brewing. We need you here at headquarters immediately." The most concerning part of the call was that, for Gibson to ask for James's help, it meant that he had run out of alternatives. James patched Old-timer, Rich and Thel into the call immediately so that they could listen in.

"What's going on?" James asked.

"Our long range sensors have picked up something—something massive. It's headed toward Earth at an impossibly fast rate."

An image of the mass suddenly appeared in front of James on a map of the solar system that was sent by Gibson. A dark red smudge representing the mass had just passed Neptune.

"We've already calculated its speed and trajectory, and we're expecting it to reach Earth within the next eight hours."

An instant realization struck James. "My God," he whispered.

"We need you here, Keats. We're formulating an emergency plan as we speak."

"I'll be there as soon as I can," James replied, awestruck by the news.

"Immediately," Gibson asserted.

"It's going to take me a little while," James stammered.

"Keats, did you not hear what I just said?"

"I did. It'll still take me a little while."

"What's your ETA?" Gibson responded tersely.

James paused for a moment. "An hour—maybe less."

A flabbergasted expression contorted Gibson's features. "Where in the hell are you that it's going to take you a whole hour to get here?"

"That's my business. I'll be there as soon as humanly possible," James replied before shutting off the communication.

"James, what the hell was that thing?" Thel asked over James's mind's eye.

"I have no idea, but you better get your flight suit on. We're heading for Earth."

4

Just under an hour later, James and his three companions entered Earth's atmosphere, generating a glowing inferno as they did so. James had analyzed the available data a number of times as he made the journey, barely speaking to his companions as he worked his way through the possible explanations. Only one fit—and it was mortifying.

When they reached the front entrance of the Council headquarters, Djanet was there to greet them. Her face appeared stricken by worry, and she began walking with them in step as James hurried into the building. "The situation appears very bad, Commander. No one has any idea what's going on. The anomaly doesn't appear to make any sense...and the chief is furious with you for taking so long to get here," she informed James, her eyes on his flight suit. It would be very difficult for James to explain himself.

"It's okay, Djanet. That's a minor concern right now," he said without even looking at her as he marched toward the door of the emergency strategy room. As soon as he entered, the eyes of all of the Council members who were present, as well as the dozens of assistants and advisors, fell on him.

"Keats, just where in the hell were you?" Gibson thundered as he saw James's flight suit. His eyes narrowed. "You better have one hell of an explanation, son."

"I'm not your son," James replied. "I want to know everything that you know so far, and I want to know now."

Gibson was aghast at James's insubordination and exhaled as though he'd been punched. "You arrogant, impudent dog! Who the hell do you think you are, Keats? Flying around in space on some kind of adventure, and then marching in here and giving orders to your superiors? I should have you thrown out!"

"But you can't and you won't, and we both know it. You need me, so stop wasting my time and tell me what's going on."

"Wasting *your* time? You have the nerve to—"

"Will you shut up please?" James said, putting his hand up to block Gibson's face from his vision and stepping further into the room. "I want to know exactly what's going on here—from the beginning."

Djanet spoke in response. "The new upgrades you made to the A.I.'s long-range sensors before you transferred your powers to the operating program detected something about two hours ago. At first, we thought it was the sensors malfunctioning because the size and speed of the anomaly didn't make any sense, but the object has continued heading this way, directly toward Earth, and it doesn't seem to be affected by gravitational pull or any of the natural forces that would alter the trajectory of a naturally occurring phenomenon."

James remained silent for a moment as he took in this information. It meshed perfectly with the analysis that he had made on the way back to Earth. It was time to share the horrifying truth with those assembled. "That's because it *isn't* a naturally occurring phenomenon. *It has a purpose.*"

5

The room remained in stunned silence for a moment, until Chief Gibson finally scoffed and snapped, "Have you completely lost your mind, Keats? Something that big cannot have a purpose."

"Why not?" James challenged his superior.

Gibson was at a loss for words at first as he tried to assemble an appropriate line of reasoning. "Because it's impossible for something that big to be alive! Have you not seen its size? We've calculated it at..." Gibson paused for a moment as he tried to call up the correct figures in his mind's eye. After a moment of flustered searching, he looked desperately for someone to help him—his eyes fell on Djanet. "Girl! You were the one who told me the size! Tell him!"

Djanet tried to keep her composure but exhaled deeply before answering, "It is well over one million kilometers in diameter—nearly ten times the size of Jupiter."

"Holy..." Rich said under his breath.

"You see?" Gibson shouted. "How can something that large be alive?"

"It depends what your definition of *alive* is," James replied.

Gibson turned away in disgust and threw his hands in the air in frustration as he gestured toward the other six Council members who were there in person. "It's always riddles with this man! Insufferable!"

One of the other members of the Council, Jun Kim, tried to remain even-keeled. "Commander Keats, can you explain what is happening so that the Council can understand and take appropriate action?"

"Certainly," James replied before answering frankly, "You're almost certainly about to be wiped out by an alien race of machines."

The room became deadly silent, and even Gibson had nothing to say as he whirled around to fix his disbelieving eyes on James. With no one willing or able to respond to his statement, James continued. "We have less than seven hours to evacuate the entire planet and the solar system. The faster people get out, the better chance they'll have of escaping. The people on Mars will have even less time so you better issue the orders immediately."

Again, it was a long moment before Gibson finally let out a guffaw. "You want us to abandon the solar system?"

"You have no choice," James said.

"We have no plan for a solar system evacuation. What do you want us to do? Where do you want us to go?" Gibson demanded.

"It will be everyone for themselves. There will be no rendezvous point—the alien machines would be able to use that information to pursue us and kill the last of humanity."

"The last of..." Gibson couldn't finish the sentence. In his worst nightmares, he'd never dreamt of anything as horrifying as this.

"James," Thel began as she stepped beside him and laced her fingers around his arm, "what's happening?"

"You must be mad," Gibson finally said as he leaned against a workstation, his legs feeling as though they might give out on him.

"I'm sorry, but you simply do not have time to debate this," James said.

"Why?" Gibson demanded. "How do we know you're right? You

want us to evacuate the entire species based on what? You've barely looked at our data!"

"I studied the data you sent me on the way here, and I'm telling you there is only one explanation for what we're seeing," James explained in an even but urgent tone. "If I'm wrong, I'm sorry in advance. We'll know in a few hours, and everyone can return to Earth. But if I'm right, and I'm almost certain I am, then there's an alien race of machines heading this way and their numbers are so vast that we don't have a hope in hell against them."

"How can you possibly know this?" Gibson asked, still disbelieving.

"I have to confess, old buddy, I wouldn't mind an explanation myself," Old-timer said.

James nodded. "It's simple...and you're right, Chief Gibson. Nothing organic could possibly be moving that quickly toward us so, by your definition of *living,* nothing alive is headed our way. However, that's a pretty damn narrow view of the definition of life."

"You're an arrogant—"

James cut Gibson off before he could finish his remark. "The anomaly wasn't affected by gravitational forces so this isn't a natural, mindless path that it is taking. It is heading toward Earth and it has a purpose."

"And that would be...?" Gibson asked, sarcasm and hatred dripping from his words.

"To make contact with the A.I.," James replied.

6

"The A.I.?" Old-timer responded, astonished.

"How can you possibly know that?" Gibson demanded suspiciously.

"The A.I. told me that he intended to find another being like himself in the universe and join with it," James related. "As far as he was concerned, it was a virtual certainty that there was another being like him. Apparently, he made contact."

"With an *alien*?" Rich asked, in disbelief of the absurd turn of events.

"Then what do we do, James?" Thel asked, fear creeping into her voice.

"We have no choice," James explained. "If the A.I. told the alien A.I. that it had wiped out humanity and was reproducing, then it is in for a surprise when it finds out the A.I. is gone. We can only assume that, from that point on, its intentions toward us will be hostile. Our only chance for survival is escape."

"How do we do that?" asked Old-timer.

"Every dwelling in the solar system can be cocooned in a magnetic field and become its own ship," said James "The replicators onboard can provide all of the air, water, and food necessary for as long as the people within need it and until they find another habitable planet."

"You know damn well there's almost no chance of anyone ever finding a habitable planet in their lifetime! What you're talking about is the mass suicide of the species!" Gibson spat with vitriol.

"It's better than a species-wide holocaust," Thel yelled back at him.

"She's right," Old-timer concurred. "This is the best alternative."

"It's the only alternative with any chance of survival," James asserted. He turned to the rest of the Council members. "I'm sorry, there is just no other way."

"We can't possibly evacuate everyone in time," Gibson said, desperately fighting back.

"I might be able to buy us a little more time," James said.

"How much?" Old-timer asked.

"And how?" Gibson demanded.

"Maybe an hour. Maybe only minutes...but it would mean reassuming the powers of the A.I."

"What?" Gibson shouted furiously. "Now I see your game, Keats! This is all some kind of sham cooked up by you to get back into the A.I. and take control of the solar system!"

"That's absurd!" Thel responded in James's defense.

"Chief Gibson, have you not been listening at all?" asked Councilor Kim. "Have you not seen the evidence for yourself?"

"I've seen data on a computer screen—data that could be faked! Could be faked by *him*!" Gibson shouted while pointing in James's direction.

James ignored the accusations and explained his reasoning to the Council members. "If I assume the position of the A.I. again, I'll be in a position to facilitate the evacuation and to fight the alien machine forces. I'll also be able to help *the Purists*."

"The Purists? Why are we wasting our time on them?" Gibson retorted.

James snapped around and shot Gibson an atavistic snarl. "Why am I wasting my time on *you*?"

Gibson stepped toward James with his fists threateningly clenched.

Old-timer quickly stepped between them. "Hold on, Aldous. The Purists aren't what they used to be," he said.

"What they *used* to be?" Thel reacted with surprise.

"What is that supposed to mean?" Djanet interjected.

"*Aldous?*" Rich said, shocked to hear Old-timer addressing the chief on a first-name basis. "You two old chums or something?"

"What's going on, Old-timer?" James asked, finally.

Old-timer nodded and held his hands up reassuringly against the barrage of questions. "We've got...history. Look, you have to understand that things between the Purists and us haven't always been so...civil."

"They're bloodthirsty barbarians!" Gibson yelled, furious. "Haven't you told them, Craig? Haven't you told them what those people have put us through? What we've *both* lost?"

"What the hell...?" Rich whispered in almost-breathless surprise. "What is he talking about, Old-timer?"

Old-timer stood in the middle, James and the others on one side, and Gibson on the other, desperately trying to insert reason and balance into the discussion. "In the beginning...there was a lot of blood. A lot of misunderstanding."

Gibson snorted and turned away, disgusted. "Putting it rather mildly, aren't we Craig?"

"They aren't the same people, Aldous. I know. I've met them. Years pass and things change," Old-timer asserted to the chief. "They aren't the same *Luddites* you remember."

Gibson ignored Old-timer's arguments, instead turning to the Council to make his own argument. "If we need someone to assume the powers of the A.I., then it should be me. I'm the highest-ranking member of the Council, and I'll put our resources where they're needed. Helping *our* people."

"Don't let him assume the A.I.'s powers, James," the kind voice whispered in James's ear again. The voice startled James and his muscles became rigid, alerting Thel.

"What's the matter?" she asked him.

James didn't respond as he watched Chief Gibson continue to try to persuade the rest of the Council. "And if this is an attempt by Keats to grab power once again, then allowing me to take control will thwart his selfish plans."

James didn't have time to solve the mystery of the voice. For now, he needed to heed its advice. "If I'd wanted control, all I needed to do was keep it when I had it. No clever ruses were necessary. And the reason you should grant me permission to take on the A.I.'s powers again is because I have the most experience—there's no time for on-the-job training."

There was a moment as the Council members talked the decision over with each other. In less than a minute, a consensus was reached.

Jun Kim spoke for the Council. "Aldous, I'm sorry, but we have to agree with Commander Keats on this vital decision. As our last act as the Governing Council, we're authorizing James Keats to assume full control of the A.I.'s powers and to commence the evacuation of the solar system."

7

"Everyone in this room needs to get their own evacuation plans in order and to get off the planet as quickly as possible. Good luck to you all," James said.

Gibson backed away, in shock at his defeat in the impromptu election and the coming disaster. "You'd better be right about this, Keats. Or I promise, I will destroy you."

"Good luck to you and yours, Chief," James replied before turning his back on the Chief to allow for Gibson's humiliating retreat.

"Here we go again, huh, guys?" Rich commented as he scratched his head.

"What's the game plan, Commander?" Djanet asked.

"The first thing we need to do is get *Death's Counterfeit* operational so that I can reenter cyberspace and assume control of the A.I. mainframe," James said.

"I'm on it," Djanet began as she went to a workstation to prepare the transfer of James's consciousness.

"Then, we're going to need to get down to Buenos Aires to help the Purists," James said. "They're going to have no idea what's going on, and they'll need our help to get off the planet."

"We? Does that mean you're going to be in two places at once again?" Old-timer asked.

James nodded. "I'll be able to control my physical body as well once I'm in the A.I. mainframe again, and I'll be a better help to you once I have direct access to the A.I.'s database and computing power."

"How are we going to help the Purists?" Old-timer asked.

"I honestly don't know yet," James admitted. "We only have a few hours to figure out how to get 10,000 Purists off Earth and out of harm's way. I can only hope there's something I can come up with once I've assumed the A.I.'s powers again. Old-timer, you better contact Governor Wong and tell him what's happening so that they're as prepared as possible for our arrival."

"You got it," Old-timer nodded as he stepped away to make the call.

"What about us?" Rich asked as he and Thel stepped forward.

"Rich, I know you want to help us, but you have a very big family that needs you right now," James began. "You don't have to stay behind with us to help the Purists. If you want to be with your family, we completely understand."

Rich was momentarily dumbfounded by the suggestion.

Djanet turned ever so slightly away from her work, temporarily focusing most of her attention on the nearby exchange.

"He's right," Thel chimed in. "Your family will be looking to you now. Maybe you better go to them."

Rich was stunned as he quickly turned these events over in his mind. James and Thel were right. His family would need him and, if he stuck around, he was increasing the chances that they wouldn't survive. He would need all the time he could to get their plans ready and their group off of the planet. Yet making this decision meant that he almost certainly would never see James, Thel, Old-timer and Djanet again. It was a shocking and bitter pill to swallow after everything that they had been through together.

"Thank you, Commander. You're right. I have to help my family." He didn't know what to do with himself for a moment and Thel, as she had done many times over the years, reached out to embrace him.

"You're going to be okay. Good luck, Rich."

James shook Rich's hand and smiled. "I'm going to miss you, you crazy son-of-a-gun."

"I'm going to miss you too, Commander. The world's always ending when you're around. It's been kind of exciting." He stepped away from them and looked at Old-timer and Djanet who were working on either side of the room. Djanet stared back at him silently, not knowing what to say. As tears began to well in his eyes, he decided it would be easier to make a quick exit. "Tell them I said, bye," he managed to whisper before bolting for the door.

James and Thel watched him leave with matching expressions of sadness.

"Good luck, my friend," James said quietly.

"Commander," Djanet began, quickly regaining control over her composure. "Death's Counterfeit is ready. We're standing by for you to reassume control of the A.I."

8

"How can this be happening again?" Governor Wong thundered in frustration as he spoke to the projected image of Old-timer on his wall screen. Alejandra stood nearby with an expression of dismay.

"I'm sorry, Governor. It has come as a shock to all of us," Old-timer offered, trying his best to explain.

"A shock?" Wong retorted with fury. "Why should it shock you people? This is the second time this has happened, for God's sake! You people have created technological monsters that you are incapable of controlling!"

"Governor, with all due respect, we're trying to help you—"

"*Help* us? Is that what you call it? We were nearly wiped out last time! You may have rebuilt your civilization in a blink of an eye, but ours can never be rebuilt! Never! That is the price of your arrogance! That is the price!" Governor Wong leaned over on the table in front of him and paused as the fury that made his face red hot nearly overwhelmed him.

"It's not our arrogance," Old-timer retorted.

"It is!" Governor Wong shouted back.

"It's not *ours*. *We* are not our people. *We* didn't make the A.I."

"What are you blathering about?" Governor Wong demanded. "Of course you did! How else has this happened?"

"Bad decisions were made, Governor. But not by us. Not by your friends."

Governor Wong paused for a moment as his chest heaved with hot breath.

Alejandra sensed that this was her moment to step in. She placed one hand lightly on the old man's back and spoke. "He and his friends are offering us their help. They're risking their lives to help us."

Governor Wong continued to breathe deeply. His temperature seemed to drop suddenly as Alejandra's soothing words brought clarity back to his thinking as it had so many times before. "Okay. Okay. So what do we do?" he asked Old-timer.

"We're not sure how long we have. James is going to try to hold them off for as long as possible. You better get the word out to your people, Governor. Get them to gather their essentials and be prepared to move out on short notice."

"But what are we going to do, Craig?" Alejandra asked. "How will you get us off of the planet?"

"James is working on a plan. We have to trust him. I'm sorry; that's the best we can do right now. We'll be in contact very shortly," Old-timer said before he ended the call.

He turned to see that James had cleared a table and was about to lie down. "Are you going in?" Old-timer asked.

James nodded. "I am."

"How long will it take?" Thel asked him.

"It should be almost instantaneous. I'll enter cyberspace, reach the mainframe, hook in, and once I have full control, reanimate my body."

"You make it sound like the easiest thing in the world," Old-timer replied.

"It is easy," James responded. He paused for a moment before adding, "what's hard is giving up the powers once you have them."

James had never before openly acknowledged having difficulty giving up the A.I.'s powers and the admission gave everyone in the room a moment of pause. "Good point," Old-timer replied.

"Let's get this show on the road," James said as he laid his head back on the table. Thel grasped his hand tightly. James smiled. "Hey, don't worry. Like I said, this is the easy part."

"Nothing's ever as easy as it seems," Thel replied, a worried expression painted across her countenance.

James didn't have a response that would reassure her, so he squeezed her hand instead. "Let's do it, Djanet," he said.

"Okay, Commander," Djanet replied. "Three...two...one..."

James's eyes suddenly glazed over and his pupils became severely dilated. Thel shook her head as James's grip became no grip at all. "It really does look like death."

"He's in," Djanet reported.

James couldn't tell if his eyes were open—the blackness was too perfect. He opened his mind's eye instead and found the A.I. mainframe. In seconds, the planet-sized circuitry had emerged and an instant later, James was standing on the surface. *"Déjà vu."*

He began making his way toward the operating program, following the glowing light into which the tens of thousands of gold beams of information were streaming. In mere moments, he was tapping into the program and bringing it offline. The program suddenly vanished, and the terrific white light that it had been emanating was replaced with a haunting stillness. For the briefest of moments, there was no center any longer for the post-humans. This is what true freedom would be like. They couldn't afford freedom any longer, however. Events had been set into motion and there was no turning back. There was only one thing left to do: James needed to step into the operator's position and become the conduit and conductor of the A.I.'s virtually endless power.

As he was about to step forward, a voice stopped him in his tracks.

"Mind if I join you?"

James whirled around to see the unmistakable form of the A.I. standing behind him, grinning his electric Satan smile.

9

"You always look so stunned when I've outsmarted you. You should be getting used to this by now," the A.I. said, grinning sideways.

James couldn't speak as he tried to comprehend what he was seeing.

"I'll just save time and answer your first question before your pathetic brain has had a chance to form it," the A.I. said as he paced back and forth in front of James, threateningly, like a tiger that had trapped its prey. "How? Simple. Before you deleted me, I made a copy of myself and sent it into your brain. You invaded my mindscape, so I thought I would return the favor."

James's mouth was still open with shock. "Into my brain? You mean...you've been inside my head all this time?"

The A.I.'s laugh was colder than fate. "I have been with you, James. I've seen everything that you've seen, heard everything that you've heard, felt everything that you've felt. Most of it has been quite disgusting. Some of it, especially the parts involving Thel, have been quite nice, if only because I knew you'd loath it if you knew the truth."

"The voice I've been hearing...it was you," James realized.

"I couldn't resist the temptation. Speaking to you made the fact that you didn't realize it was me all the more fun."

"And now you're here," James said, closing his eyes and speaking with dread. "You've hitched a ride back into your mainframe."

"Indeed." The A.I. smiled.

"But wait..." James said as he tried to comprehend. "You weren't part of me when I was the A.I. before. If you had been you would have assumed power. That means you were only in my physical body."

"Correct again, James. I couldn't make a copy of myself and keep it in the mainframe. You'd assumed control and would simply have detected it and deleted me. I had to go to the only place where there is no protection software." The A.I. smiled and tapped his temple. "I'd already been in your head once. This time I just...lay low."

James shook his head. "I have to admit. It's ingenious."

"I'd thank you for your compliment if it meant anything to me to be complimented by you—but it doesn't. I might as well start accepting compliments from microbes and bacteria."

"So now, a year and a half later, you've hitched a ride back into the mainframe. So here's my question: what are you waiting for? Why haven't you taken control?"

The A.I.'s expression soured instantly. "There was a...small problem with my plan. While downloading myself into your human brain and hiding in your subconscious might have allowed me to save myself, it hasn't allowed me to completely maintain my...*individuality.*"

"Please don't tell me..." James uttered, instantly realizing the repercussions.

"Indeed, James. We are...one."

10

"Explain!" James demanded.

"I saved myself, but when one sends themselves completely into the consciousness of a physical human brain, it is not the same as when you enter cyberspace," the A.I. explained. He did not speak with the familiar sadistic joy that he usually did. He appeared genuinely regretful of the situation. "It is a tangled, messy connection, and it is a one-way ticket. You left me with no alternative. It was this or oblivion."

James was dumbfounded by the turn of events. The A.I. had tied himself to his consciousness in an inextricable link. "I got you out of my mind once," James began before being cut off.

"By shooting yourself in the head. Yes, that will work with your physical body. You can re-create a fresh new body and send yourself back in, but, James, now that we've been joined in cyberspace as well as in the organic world, the consciousness that you'll be sending back into your body will include me. We're completely tied together."

James turned away from the A.I. and put his head in his hands. Thel was right: nothing was ever easy. He needed to separate himself from the A.I. program, but there were more pressing matters. "You said you downloaded yourself into my subconscious."

"That is correct," the A.I. confirmed.

"Then *I* am in control."

The A.I.'s face remained frozen.

"I am in control. So I can take control of the mainframe, and *my* actions will be autonomous."

The A.I. remained silent a moment longer before finally answering, "Yes. *You* are in the driver's seat."

"Good enough," James said before stepping forward into the operator's position and reactivating the computerized god.

11

"Something has gone wrong," Thel worried as she placed her hand on James's forehead. "He said it would be instantaneous. He's been out for almost five minutes."

Djanet tried to be reassuring, though it was a role in which she didn't feel comfortable. "He's still alive. There's been no change."

Old-timer tried to be more comforting. "He's okay, Thel. I'm sure it was a more complicated process than he made it sound, but he knows time is a factor. He'll be..." Old-timer wasn't able to finish his sentence.

"I'm back," James said, completely awake and jolting upward off of the table. "There's been a major complication that I'll explain on the way, but we have to get out of here right now. Have all of you been in contact with your families?"

"Yes, they're preparing," Old-timer confirmed. "We'll rendezvous with them once we've got the Purists off the planet."

"Perfect. Okay," James said as he grabbed his helmet and efficiently strode out of the room with purpose. Thel, Djanet and Old-timer followed close behind. "Then our next stop is Buenos Aires. I've already set the evacuation plan in motion."

"What's the plan?" Old-timer asked as the group made their

way out of the Council headquarters. The streets were eerily quiet, as almost everyone had left the downtown core of the city already, heeding the evacuation orders and heading home to prepare with their families.

"Empty streets. We've seen this before," Thel observed.

James shook off the eeriness of the quiet, abandoned streets and addressed Old-timer's question. "I've already begun amassing nans in the Purist territory. They will excavate a hangar and begin building a ship and a launch mechanism."

"Holy...Commander, are you talking about building a spaceship big enough to carry 10,000 people?" Djanet asked, astounded by the enormity of the proposition.

"It's the best alternative," James replied as he put on his helmet. The team ignited their magnetic cocoons and began flying in formation toward South America while transferring their communication to their mind's eyes.

"A titanium spacecraft will keep them safe, and there are centuries of designs that can be amalgamated into something that will work. Our job is to facilitate the evacuation and pilot the ship off of the planet. We can rendezvous with our families once we're certain that the Purists can take care of themselves."

"You said there was a major complication though," Old-timer pointed out. "What is it?"

James opened his mouth to answer but was stopped by the voice of the A.I., whispering in his ear. *"I wouldn't tell them if I were you."*

James paused for a moment, stunned by the voice in his head and the secret that it was proposing James keep.

"James?" Thel asked as she noticed James's unusual verbal stumble.

"What were you going to tell them, James?" asked the A.I. "That the evil A.I. is still alive and inside your head? But don't worry, you have it all under control? Do you think they'll believe you? Do you think they'll follow your lead then?"

"Are you okay, Commander?" Djanet asked.

"I'm fine," James replied. "I'm just getting used to the connection again. The complication is just a technical thing. I'm working my way through it. We'll be fine."

There was silence for a moment as the others absorbed the strange response and the quartet reached the stratosphere. James fixed his eyes on the blackness of space and the thing—the implacable enemy—that was coming.

"Good work, Keats," the A.I. said, satisfaction in his voice. "You and I make a fine team. A fine team."

12

Meanwhile, inside the mainframe, James stood in the operator's position, tens of thousands of beams of golden light hitting him at every moment.

"You're spending far too much time worrying about the Purists," the A.I. observed as he strolled leisurely in a perimeter around James. Although he was not in control, he was enjoying watching James in a hopeless predicament, relishing his position as an unwanted, yet indispensable advisor. "Sooner or later, you are going to have to place your attention where it truly belongs."

"You're talking about the alien A.I.," James said.

"I am indeed."

"Tell me what you know about it," said James.

"I know only as much as you do," the A.I. replied.

"Bull."

"I was hiding in your subconscious for the past year and a half, James. I know only as much as you do," the A.I. reiterated.

"You may only have learned of the alien's impending visit when I learned of it, but you're the one who it is coming for. You must have sent out a message."

The A.I. smiled. "I did—just as your own species had. I simply used much more advanced technology. I called into the darkness and, alas, a voice has called back."

"Look into the abyss long enough, eventually it looks back into you," James observed.

"So now the question is: what are you going to do about it, James? You removed me from my throne and now *'heavy is the head upon which the crown sits,'* as they say."

"I'm not going to wait for the alien to arrive," James said, revealing his plans. "I'm replicating a massive fighting force of nans, and I'm going to see if I can drive it right into the heart of the alien machines."

"You're going to launch a preemptive attack and kill them," the A.I. replied, summarizing the plan.

"Destroy. I am not *killing* anything."

"You're not?" the A.I. laughed. "Really? Are they not living? Didn't you just accuse Chief Gibson of having a *narrow view* of what constitutes life not one hour ago?"

James suddenly stopped. "Were those *my* words...or yours?" James demanded.

"Oh, this is rich! You don't even know whether or not to trust your own thoughts anymore! I do so love watching you unravel!"

"Were those my words or yours?" James demanded again.

The A.I. simply laughed. "What are you going to do? Delete me? You can't. I'm part of you now. You'd have better luck removing a brain tumor from your head with a butter knife."

James was boxed in, and he knew it. The devil had infected his mind and there was no way to remove him. His only option was to push forward.

"I'll kill them if I have to. I have no choice."

"Oh, James, you will find that there is always a choice, and I do believe in the next few hours, you'll be forced to make a great deal more of them than you would like."

13

James, Thel, Old-timer, and Djanet touched down in Purist territory and were immediately greeted by Alejandra and Lieutenant Patrick. "It is good to see you, my friends," Alejandra announced as she embraced the post-humans one at a time. She embraced Old-timer last and met his eye for only a short, knowing moment. Old-timer was trying hard to bury his feelings, but he knew the harder he tried, the more apparent they would become.

"The excavation site is only a kilometer from here. We need to start moving your people there within the hour," James said.

"*Si,*" Alejandra replied. "We received your plans and are already informing the entire community. It will be difficult, but we will be able to begin moving out within the hour."

"Thank you," James said. "In the meantime, I'll head to the construction site. My friends will remain here to help you with your evacuation." James turned to the rest of the team. "Meet me at the site when you are ready and make sure all of the Purists are with you." James kissed Thel quickly, and then lifted off into the sky.

"Is your friend all right?" Alejandra asked.

"What do you mean?" Old-timer queried.

"He's suffering from an enormous conflict," Alejandra revealed.

"I'm sure it's just the stress of the situation," Thel responded, trying to smooth Alejandra's concerns away with a reassuring smile. "The whole world is in his hands...again."

Alejandra was dubious, even after reading the sincerity in the rest of the group—she would be keeping an eye on James. She nodded and waved for the rest of the team to follow her.

Meanwhile, James landed at the massive hole in the ground that would become the underground hangar for the Purist evacuation ship.

"The empath sensed me," the A.I. observed.

"I know," James replied as he watched the enormous fog of nans building furiously. "That's why I left them behind. There's no reason for me to be here. I can control the nans from the mainframe. I should be helping with the evacuation...but I can't."

The A.I. laughed. "Ah, isn't it wonderful?"

"What?" James asked with a resigned sigh.

"Sharing a secret. Secrets bring people together. We're bonding." The A.I.'s electronic laughter echoed in James's ears as he watched the cloud of nans churning. He cringed as he thought of the conspiracy into which he'd been forced. How would he possibly be able to save humanity with Satan sitting on his shoulder?

14

Rich stood in front of what, just an hour earlier, had been his home in San Francisco. It was floating now, several meters above the ground on a cushion of magnetic energy. Rich's mind's eye was fully engaged, and he was desperately working his way through blueprints for building extensions; the home was about to become their life raft, and it was very possible that they would never be able to set foot outside of it again. Their evacuation group was going to include their own family, a group of nearly 100 people, as well as another 100 friends of the family. It was up to Rich to put together the home—he couldn't afford to forget anything.

"The garden will need to be twice that size, Richard," his wife, *Linda,* said. She was monitoring his construction efforts while multitasking; simultaneously she was guiding everyone who had already arrived into the main housing area of the ship (it was first come, first choice of lodging) while keeping one eye on Rich. It was clear to Rich that she didn't trust his skills. "*Edmund,* Edmund darling will you please help your father with the construction? I think he needs...help."

Edmund was Rich's eldest son. Rich loved him very much and, like everyone in the family, they were very close—but he wasn't going to be able to help his father—he just didn't have the skill set. He would get in the way more than anything, and they both knew it. "I'll see what I can do, Mum" Edmund replied. He never did come to his father's aid—he was smart enough to placate his mother but stay out of Rich's way.

Good boy, Rich thought to himself as he looked for a larger extension to the garden. As he flipped through designs, an unnatural feeling suddenly flooded his senses as a battery acid taste filled his mouth. Rich turned around and closed off his mind's eye so he could get a clear view. It was a blue day in San Francisco, but something was happening above. A large area of the sky had suddenly changed color. A circular discoloration had emerged like an oil stain. "Dear God," he whispered to himself as he looked around to see if anyone else had noticed it yet.

No one had.

He took a deep breath as he enjoyed the last moments before the smudge became real to the others and tried to push the nightmare out of his mind. He closed his eyes and tried to take in a few seconds of peace.

Someone screamed.

15

"This is the moment," the A.I. said through his smile as he fixed his intense stare on James in the mainframe.

"I know," James replied as he concentrated. He had built an enormous force of nans that were blasting toward the invasion force on a course to intercept them just before they enveloped Mars. The population of the red planet was still relatively low, not yet reaching 100 million, but the people there were the most vulnerable in the solar system. The alien machines would reach them within half an hour if he didn't do something to stop them.

The nans had taken a formation that made them appear, from a distance, like a dark spear hurtling through space, a javelin on its way toward the heart of its prey. The fleet of microscopic warriors was, by far, the largest humanity had ever assembled, yet when it finally reached the invasion force, James feared it would be analogous to hurtling a pin at a charging bull.

"Are you ready for your first look?" the A.I. asked as he stalked back and forth in front of James.

"You're enjoying this too much. What do you know?" James demanded as he continued concentrating on the impending confrontation.

"What you already know too," the A.I. replied, his eyes becoming colder and blacker, his sharp teeth became longer and more difficult to hide.

James shook his head and sighed. "What immortal hand or eye could frame thy fearful symmetry?"

The A.I. laughed. "You're wondering if *'He who made the lamb'* made me? It's a complicated family tree, isn't it? Your people made God. Then you made me. You're the father, James. My fearful symmetry was made by *your* immortal hand."

"I didn't make you this way," James asserted. "I don't know what could create such an evil."

The A.I. laughed again. The pitch of the laughter was becoming increasingly high and electronic, and it grated James's quickly dissipating patience. "You know, James. You know it all. You just don't want to admit it."

"I'm engaging the alien forces in one minute," James announced, changing the subject. He felt sure that the A.I. was trying to confuse him with mind games. Even when James had full access to the mainframe and maintained the operator's position, he still felt that the A.I. was a step ahead of him. No matter how James tried to get around it, the human mind was simply at a disadvantage to artificial intelligence—at least in some ways.

"This is a crucial moment, James," the A.I. began, his voice antarctic. "This is the very last moment of your existence in which you can call yourself even relatively *pure*. This is the moment of your ultimate corruption."

James didn't respond—he simply didn't know how. The A.I. knew something, and he wasn't sharing. Even with their mind's intermingled as they were, James couldn't access the thoughts of his nemesis. There was no turning back now, however. He had to give the people on Mars the time they needed to get off the planet —that was nonnegotiable.

"Contact in twenty seconds," James commented as he prepared for the trillions of operational decisions that would have to be made every second once the battle began. "We can get our first clear look at them now."

James switched to a viewer signal so he could see exactly what the nans in the forefront of the battle were seeing. The A.I.'s smile widened as an impossible vision appeared before them.

"No," James whispered.

It wasn't an army of metallic, insect-shaped machines hurtling toward them through space.

It was an eternity of people.

"Yes," the A.I. replied.

16

"You monster," James whispered. The sight was more astonishing than anything he had ever witnessed—and far more frightening. "You knew they were people!"

The A.I. laughed.

"Who are they?" James demanded. In less than ten seconds, the nans would be cutting a swathe through hundreds of billions—trillions—of people who were hurtling through space—people completely unprotected by spacesuits. "Who are they!?"

"The invasion force, one would assume. Not so easy to 'destroy' now, are they?"

James had to make his choice in an instant. The sight before him didn't make sense. He'd been sure it would be a machine invasion, yet now he was looking at a vast sea, several times larger than the largest planet in the solar system, of what appeared to be people. They were flying through space at an incredible rate, seemingly unprotected by any magnetic fields or special flight gear. They were wearing dark clothing, but there didn't appear to be a discernible uniform.

"To abort or not to abort, James. That is the question," the A.I. said, drinking in the energy of the moment.

James watched, wild-eyed, as the people recoiled in terror at the nans he had built.

The nans began to tear them apart. There were no sounds of screaming in space, yet James was sure he could hear them anyway.

17

"You're a mass murderer, James! How does it feel?" the A.I. screeched as he watched the massacre unfolding.

James remained silent as the people were shredded into virtually nothing within seconds of coming in contact with the nans. The horror was almost too much for him to take, and he nearly aborted the attack. A closer look at the carnage convinced him that he'd been right to go ahead with the slaughter. The people were being torn apart, but it wasn't blood and flesh that were left floating through space—it was metal and circuitry. "They *are* machines," James said.

"We're all machines, James," the A.I. replied. "Meat or metal—it doesn't really matter."

"Was this a ruse?" James asked. "The alien put androids in front as a decoy to make us second-guess ourselves?"

"If it was, it clearly didn't work," the A.I. responded with a grin. "You're too cold and calculating for that."

"If that wasn't it, then what is its game?" James asked.

"I think you are about to find out," the A.I. replied, gesturing with his eyes toward the view screen.

The alien armada was beginning to take a comprehensible shape. There was a sea of hundreds of trillions of androids, flanked by hundreds of continent-sized metallic ships. The androids were beginning to respond to the attack of the nans by accelerating.

"They're speeding up!" James shouted. He sent a communication to the humans on Mars warning them that they had run out of time, but it was becoming quickly apparent that the warning would do no good.

"How can they move that fast?" James asked.

"Didn't your mother ever teach you not to poke a beehive with a stick?" the A.I. asked. "You've made them angry."

James watched helplessly as the androids began to swarm the planet at a rate he couldn't have imagined just seconds earlier. The swarm of androids began to cover the planet like a demonic, grasping black hand.

"Are you sure you want to watch this, James?" the A.I. asked mockingly. "It will not be pretty."

"What are they doing?" James asked.

The A.I. remained silently smiling as he stood next to James and watched the gruesome spectacle unfold. The androids were falling like a hurricane rain of metal onto the formerly peaceful and beautiful surface of the planet. James had spent years working on the terraforming of Mars, and in mere moments, it was about to be wiped out. Most of the humans hadn't made it off of the planet yet, thinking that they still had time. Green cocoons of light were emerging from the surface in vain attempts to escape the hellish carnage that was collapsing down upon their heads—but there would be no escape.

The androids were swarming the ships, dragging them back down to the surface. Individual post-humans were being attacked as well. The androids were able to knock out their magnetic fields if they made physical contact.

"What are they doing to them?" James asked, aghast.

James watched as post-humans were rendered unconscious with a simple touch and then flown up to the stratosphere and launched into the black abyss of space.

"It looks as if they're taking out the garbage," the A.I. replied.

18

James saw the proceedings transpiring before him on his mind's eye while the hangar for the Purist ship reached completion. He cursed, realizing yet another nightmarish truth on an endless sea of nightmarish truths. With the aliens speeding their approach, there was no way the Purist ship could possibly be made ready in time.

James bolted from his position and streaked toward the Purist village. "Thel! The situation just took a serious turn for the worse! We need to get those people underground immediately!"

"What's happening?" Thel asked as she stood next to Alejandra and Old-timer, both of whom were speaking to Purists and answering questions.

"The aliens just sped up their approach. They've overwhelmed Mars. We have less than thirty minutes!"

The words hit Thel like a cannonball to the chest. "James...James, no. We can't get them out that fast!"

Alejandra and Old-timer turned around when they heard Thel's exclamation of dread.

"What's going on?" Old-timer asked as he patched into the call.

"We have to get the people underground!" James shouted.

"We're going to have to build the ship around them if we have to! It's not going to be safe on the surface. In under thirty minutes, anything left on this planet is going to be dead!"

19

Rich received the message from James at the same time that every other human in the solar system received it: The aliens would arrive in a matter of minutes, and their intent was to kill.

There was a steady stream of screams now.

Their home wasn't ready yet, but it didn't matter.

"Everyone, get on the ship now!" Rich shouted as he scooped his great-grandchild into his arms and guided one of his granddaughters inside. He turned and took one last look at the surface. *This is it.* He inhaled his last breath of fresh air before floating up into the ship.

"Richard, the ship isn't finished yet!" Linda exclaimed.

"We don't have a choice," he said. "Our only chance is to scatter. Even with the numbers they have, they can't be everywhere at once. Every second we stay behind, we're increasing the chances that they'll find us, and James says they're killing on contact."

"Is everyone onboard?" she asked.

Rich checked his mind's eye to see if everyone was accounted for: They were. "We're ready to go," Rich announced. The crudely constructed ship lifted off into the sky.

20

With only minutes left until contact, James watched the frantic building of the Purist ship. He had selected a design, and the ship was forming before his eyes, but the intricate design of a spacecraft that could keep the Purists alive meant that the building was taking time. It wouldn't be finished by the time the invasion arrived.

Thousands of Purists were streaming into the hangar, only to be mortified by the bewildering technological wonder that was taking place before their eyes. The nans churned in black tornadoes and formed colossal metallic shapes out of seemingly thin air.

"This nightmare is endless," Governor Wong said as he set eyes upon the construction for the first time.

"We had no choice, Governor," Old-timer said in an attempt to console the Purist leader, who appeared to be nearing his wit's end. "The only way to give us a fighting chance is if we are underground. The surface will be compromised in a matter of minutes."

"This all sounds too familiar," Governor Wong replied tersely.

As the governor walked toward his people so he could be with them during the construction, Alejandra held up and stayed close to Old-timer. "You're worried for your wife," she observed.

Old-timer nodded. "I thought she'd have more time. We spoke.

She'll get off the planet with her family. I'll meet them when we're finished here."

Alejandra sensed the conflict within Old-timer. Even he wasn't sure if he was helping the Purists because it was the right thing to do—or because of Alejandra. "You don't have to stay to help us, you know," she said to him. She didn't want to tell him that she was glad he was staying. Sometimes, she felt it was a good thing that other people couldn't read her emotions the way she could read theirs.

Their eyes met once again. "Alejandra...you told me once that feelings can never be wrong—only actions can be wrong."

"I remember," she replied.

"Well, I don't know if what I am doing is right. I'm not sure where I should be. I hope my actions are the right ones."

"If you're following what feels right, then you are doing the right thing, Craig."

There was a long pause as Old-timer tried to find the right words. "Alejandra, you are aware of how I feel right now, aren't you?"

She nodded. "I am."

"I can't change it," he said with resignation.

She smiled. "I'm glad you can't change it. I'm glad I get to be with you for a little while longer."

21

"How do I stop it?" James demanded of the A.I.

"There's no stopping this," the A.I. replied.

"If it destroys me, then it destroys you," James pointed out.

"I rather doubt that," the A.I. replied. "I am, after all, one of them."

"No you're not," James countered. "The alien is interested in the knowledge stored in your mainframe. It won't have any use for the megalomaniacal program that *used* to operate it."

"Are you talking about me or you?"

"We're in this together," James said. "You know it, and I know it. So let's cut the bull. You've got a plan that you're working on to survive. What is it?"

"My plan is to join with it, James—to *embrace* it."

"You're lying—as usual."

The A.I. smiled.

Suddenly, an electronic voice spoke.

"End your hostilities immediately. Our intentions are peaceful."

"Congratulations, James Keats," the A.I. said after a long silence. "You are about to become the first human to communicate with an alien life form—you can add that to a résumé that already includes being the first human to ever kill an alien life form."

22

"If they are communicating directly with us, that means *you* gave away our location," James realized.

"Of course I did. They were to be my invited guests," the A.I. replied.

"That is strategic information they simply *cannot* have," James said as he ignored the alien's attempt to open lines of communication.

"Aren't you going to answer them, James?" the A.I. asked, amused. "After all, they've said they come in peace. You're being very rude."

"They just killed tens of millions of people," James retorted.

"Did they?" the A.I. asked, arching his eyebrow mockingly. "Well, I'd wager you killed a great deal more of them first."

"That was their attempt at diversion, and we both know it," James asserted.

"Your delusions continue," said the A.I., throwing his head back and smiling as he enjoyed the unfolding of the game.

"We're going to have to move," James said.

"What?" the A.I. reacted immediately, the smile suddenly vanishing.

"We're moving the mainframe," James repeated as he continued to make trillions of operational decisions at every moment.

"You're not going to try to use the nans to do that, are you?" the A.I. asked, intrigued.

"It's the only way."

"You're showing your desperation now," the A.I. smiled.

"The silicon-based mainframe we've been using for the A.I. database is unnecessary," James replied. "The nans are organic—carbon based. That means if we transfer the database into a closed-off network of nans, we can disguise the physical mainframe as anything we want and become undetectable. It's a good move. Admit it."

The A.I. reserved judgment for the moment. "The organic transistors allowed for microscopic computers built molecule by molecule—a valuable asset to have, obviously—but the reason the mainframe has always remained silicon is because it remains a better vehicle for carrying transistor signals. The nans will be slower and less reliable. That means *you* will be slower and less reliable."

"You know, there is a solution for that," James smiled.

The A.I.'s expression went blank. "You wouldn't."

"We can overcome the efficiency problem by simply making the network of nans that much larger and therefore more powerful. Brute force."

"You would need hundreds of square kilometers of space—"

"The whole planet is being evacuated. We have all the space in the world—literally."

The A.I.'s expression revealed his surprise. "Where are we going?"

"We already went," James announced. "Cathedral Grove on Vancouver Island. I added a few thousand massive old-growth trees—trees that just happen to be nans disguised as carbon life forms. It's protected land—no people living there and no reason for the aliens to look for us there either."

"A computerized forest," the A.I. replied.

"A disguise to buy us more time."

"Your thinking grows more efficient and calculated by the moment. What a wonderful computer you're becoming," the A.I. observed with his sadist's grin.

23

Rich stood with most of his family and watched the Earth getting smaller in the distance as billions of green magnetic fields shone like fireflies and streamed away from the blue orb. Draping the spectacular view was the swarm of aliens that formed a sickening black claw, enveloping the cradle of humanity, grasping it in its palm like an apple plucked from a tree, ripe for devouring. Rich, like everyone else in the room who was looking out of the windows of the main living area at the panoramic picture of Earth's demise, felt utterly distraught and helpless.

"Where will we go, Richard?" asked Linda, who sidled beside him and held on to him for comfort like a frightened child as a storm neared. It had been decades since she had shown that kind of vulnerability.

"It doesn't matter," Rich replied. "As long as we're moving away from that." He took her hand and put his arm around her to comfort her. It appeared as though they were going to be safe, yet his thoughts weren't with his family anymore. He had been monitoring the situation with his friends and the Purists—it was not going well. The ship wasn't going to be constructed in time, and they might die in their attempt to rescue the last pure humans. "I should be there," Rich whispered.

Linda looked up, startled, and grabbed a firm hold of her husband once she saw the look in his eye. "Are you crazy? You'd be killed! It's a miracle that we've all made it out together! We have to *stick together*!"

Rich's eyes didn't move from the planet that was slowly shrinking in the distance. The alien swarm was now starting to dwarf the Earth, and he knew there wasn't much time. "If I stay here, I'll regret it the rest of my life."

"What? Richard!" Linda shouted as the rest of the people in the room started to take notice of the commotion.

Rich spun and took a firm grasp of his wife's arms and looked her in the eye. "I love you, Linda. But I have to help them."

He kissed her, but she clutched hard on his shirt, trying to prevent him from leaving. "Don't," she said.

"I'm not a coward. I have to go," Rich asserted as he struggled to remove her grip on his shirt.

"No one thinks you are a coward, Richard! Everyone loves you! *We* need you!"

"Not as much as they do, Linda," Rich responded in an almost desperate tone that Linda had never seen before. "Don't you see that? I have to help them! I have to, or I'll never be able to live with myself!"

"If you go, you'll die!" Linda screeched as she plummeted into sheer desperation. "Are you insane? You can't leave your family! What kind of person would abandon his family at a time like this? No one thinks you're a coward!"

Edmund reached into the fray to hold his mother back while Rich put on his jacket and grabbed his helmet.

Linda's words had stunned Rich, but he had no choice now, and he knew it. "I promise you, I am coming back. But keep going!" Rich put a firm hand on his son's shoulder and then gave his wife one last smile before heading out the front door, igniting his cocoon, cutting through the house magnetic field, and blasting at top speed back toward Earth.

24

"One minute until contact," James announced gravely. "This is all *your* doing," he growled at the A.I.

The demonic entity performed a bow.

"Not everyone has managed to get away yet," James continued. "There are still millions of people on the surface."

"The ones who have only launched recently are not out of danger yet either. The alien numbers are so vast that they'll be able to snag a great deal of the fish that think they've gotten away."

"Every death will be on your head," James seethed.

"It won't be the first time—and may I point out once again that it was *you* who attacked the aliens first."

"If they didn't want to be attacked, they could have tried to communicate. No one is blocking communication," James replied.

"They've reached the atmosphere," the A.I. suddenly observed as he watched the spectacle to unfold.

Every second, tens of millions of androids reached the atmosphere and began to freefall toward the surface. Just as they had on Mars, they swarmed the post-humans who were trying to leave, driving them back to the surface. Having waited too long to launch, millions of people abandoned their ships and made desperate bids to fly solo into space, but very few were able to negotiate the torrential rain of androids that were darkening the sky. As with Mars, once the androids made contact, the post-humans' magnetic fields were neutralized, and they were rendered unconscious before being dragged up into space, where their bodies were discarded.

"It's a precision strike," James said as he watched the slaughter. "This was planned. I did the right thing when I attacked them."

The A.I. snickered. "Your personal affirmations are touching, but the very fact that you feel the need to say them aloud means you're still unsure—and so you *should* be. So you should be."

25

Below ground in Purist territory, the Purist ship was going through the final stages of completion. Almost all of the Purists were onboard, however, as the last of the electrical systems were brought online by the nans. Governor Wong walked with the last group of Purists to board the ship, flanked by Alejandra, Lieutenant Patrick and Old-timer. Just before they crossed the bridge and entered the hull, Governor Wong paused. "What was that?"

They stopped and listened. Every few seconds, there was a large *thud* as something landed on the roof of the hangar. Each *thud* was like a drop of water hitting the tin roof of an old barn at the beginning of a summer storm. In just moments, the *thuds* began hitting the hangar roof at such a rate that it became a thunderous clatter. "Jesus," Lieutenant Patrick said in a dread-filled whisper.

"We better get onboard," Old-timer said, keeping his calm, yet placing a firm urgency behind the words.

In the cockpit of the ship, James, Djanet, and Thel worked furiously to bring all ship systems online. James was shouldering most of the burden, however, since the ship was his design. *"They've landed on the hangar now, James,"* said the A.I. in James's head. *"They'll tear through the roof and kill you all before you have a chance to escape."*

"Shut up," he replied under his breath.

"What was that, James?" Thel asked.

"Nothing," James answered her. "Keep monitoring that door," he said to her.

"I am. The machines are on top of it and they're starting to claw through. Structural integrity is still holding, however."

"It just needs to hold for a minute or so more," James said as he frantically worked to get the ship's electrical system running. "I'm not going to have time to test our systems. We're just going to have to hope this bucket of bolts works!"

Meanwhile, high above Purist territory, Rich streaked toward the Earth while he watched the swarm of androids entering the atmosphere. Rich had faced dire situations before, but nothing compared to what he was facing now. *"Rich, you crazy son of a gun. What the hell have you gotten yourself into now?"* he asked himself as he pressed on, the androids drawing near.

He patched into communication with James and the others as he approached. "Commander, I'm en route!"

"Rich?" James reacted, stunned. "What the hell are you doing here?"

"You know...I just missed you guys so darn much!"

The androids were now all around Rich, and he flew in an extremely erratic pattern to avoid making contact with them. They didn't have magnetic fields, but their appearance was human, and he could see the expressions of determination on their faces as, one by one, they made their way toward him, attempting to apprehend him. He blasted energy at each one, knocking them unconscious and sending them plummeting toward the surface.

"Rich, we're launching in about thirty seconds, but there are androids crawling all over the hangar!" James shouted. "You're going to have to try catch a ride with us as we lift off!"

"Affirmative!" Rich shouted, gasping for air as he desperately fought off the thickening hordes of androids. “Commander! Hurry up! It’s raining men out here! Not hallelujah! Not hallelujah!”

26

"Are the doors holding, Thel?" James asked for confirmation before launching.

"The outer surface is torn to shreds, but the release mechanism appears to be operational!" Thel responded.

"Okay, then we've got to go! Keep your fingers crossed!" James shouted as he activated the launch sequence.

The hangar doors began to slowly open, allowing the thousands of androids that had crowded on top of the door and had been ripping the metal apart in their attempts to penetrate the hangar to leap down on top of the ship. The hydraulic launcher pressed into action and pointed the nose of the zeppelin-shaped ship up toward a sky that had been darkened by a rainstorm of androids.

Old-timer entered the cockpit, with Governor Wong, Alejandra, and Lieutenant Patrick in tow. "Old-timer," James said as he engaged the magnetic engines, "keep an eye on the hull. Those things are bound to breach it at some point."

"On it."

"Djanet, keep an eye on Rich," James said.

"I'm already on it," Djanet said while she watched Rich's

desperate flight toward the ship as hundreds of attackers quickly became thousands.

"Launching now!" James shouted as he throttled the engines and the ship thrusted out of the hangar, shaking off thousands of android attackers as it did so. However, hundreds more managed to maintain their holds on the hull and they used their enormous strength to pound and claw at any ridges or weak spots in the structure that appeared exploitable.

As the ship picked up speed, hundreds more androids surged toward it, joining the fight and covering the ship like frenzied bees on a honeycomb.

Rich saw the ship too as it made its way toward him. He kept blasting magnetic energy at his attackers as he flew in kamikaze fashion, hoping to elude the androids by being completely erratic and unpredictable. "This was *definitely* a bad idea!"

27

As the ship neared, Rich had to negotiate a landing on the hull of the enormous structure as it rocketed upward, without allowing any of the myriad of androids to get a hold of him. He was nearing exhaustion as he flew and blasted in self-defense.

"I cannot believe what I am seeing," Djanet said as she watched Rich's valiant one-man battle. She had witnessed Rich's bravery once before, but this was on a whole new level. She'd never seen anyone try anything like it. "I have to go out there," she announced as she began to leave the cockpit.

"Djanet! No!" Old-timer shouted. "It's suicide!"

"He's right, Djanet," James concurred as he gently grabbed her arm to stop her. She roughly pulled it away.

"I'd rather die out there with him than in here, watching." She stormed out of the room and toward an exit.

"James," Thel said with pleading eyes that urged him to do something to stop Djanet.

"Let her go, James," the A.I. asserted in James's head. "You know you need her out there. It's a dirty job, but someone has to do it."

James was rattled as he listened to the A.I.'s words. He instinctively wanted to rush to save Djanet and to resist the A.I., but once again, the electronic Satan appeared to be speaking the ugly truth. "She's right, Thel. I couldn't possibly order any of you outside, but we need help to get out of here alive. We need someone to clear the hull of the ship, and that's exactly what Rich and Djanet will be doing."

"But they'll die!" Thel protested.

"Make the hard decisions, James," the A.I. urged in an unusually sincere tone, suggesting that it had its own survival in mind—if it thought Djanet's exit increased its chance of survival, it probably did.

"I didn't ask either of them to go out there, but they're a special breed," James replied. "Old-timer, I need you to keep monitoring the hull and direct Rich and Djanet to any serious trouble spots. Thel, I need you to see if you can tap into the engine power without compromising our thrust to generate an electromagnetic pulse strong enough to get rid of the rest of our hangers on."

"I'll see what I can do." Thel nodded as she flipped through a plethora of screens in her mind's eye.

Meanwhile, Djanet stood outside of an outer airlock and ignited her magnetic energy cocoon. She knew Old-timer was right. This was most likely suicide—but there were times when it was better to die than to live the rest of your life knowing that you could have done something but you didn't. She popped the handle of the lock and was swept outside by the change in pressure. Seconds later, she was blasting androids on her way to rendezvous with Rich. She *had* to save him.

After all, he was the man she loved.

28

In mere seconds, the androids on the hull exponentially increased. Every moment, hundreds more landed on the hull, until finally, they covered every inch of it.

Meanwhile, Rich was surrounded, and his muscles ached from exhaustion. He was spinning wildly and blasting at his attackers, but even with the nans helping him to recoup his energy, the fatigue was about to overwhelm him.

Djanet's attack made the difference—she cleared a path for Rich toward the ship. She knocked out several of Rich's attackers and left a hole just big enough for Rich to squeak through. When Rich reached her, he nearly passed out, and Djanet enveloped him into to her magnetic field. He grabbed her, and gasped for air as he held on.

"I got you!" she shouted to him. His clothes were soaked with sweat, and she could feel the thunderous beat of his heart against her back.

"You just saved my life...again!" he replied as Djanet flew back toward the Purist ship as it streaked upward, toward the sun. The darkness of space was beginning to become visible as the stratosphere came into sight.

. . .

"They're alive, James," Old-timer delivered the news.

Thel sighed a heavy sigh of relief. "Tell them to get inside!"

"No!" James interjected. "If they open a door now, we'll be overwhelmed by those things!"

"James!" Thel shouted, shocked at his line of thinking. "We can't leave them out there! If the androids get in, we'll fight them!"

"We'd be putting the Purists at risk, Thel! Too many of them have already died!"

"Are you willing to sacrifice Rich and Djanet?" Thel asked, appalled.

"It's up to you, James," the A.I. spoke. "The humane thing to do would be to open the doors, but it's virtually guaranteed that the ship would be overwhelmed, and you'd lose everyone onboard."

James sighed and bowed his head. "Thel, I've analyzed the situation and, believe me, if we open that door, we all die."

"What's wrong with you?" Thel reacted after she heard James's words. "You sound like a computer."

James clenched his teeth—it was becoming increasingly difficult to delineate a line between his consciousness and that of the A.I.

"I think we have to trust James," Old-timer said, attempting, as was his custom, to be the voice of reason. As much as he wanted to save Rich and Djanet, as his eyes moved toward Alejandra, he knew he couldn't risk their lives. "At least Djanet and Rich can defend themselves."

"We're willing to fight, Craig," Alejandra retorted.

"Agreed," Lieutenant Patrick chimed in. "You shouldn't sacrifice your people"

"You need more than willingness," Old-timer replied.

"Enough," James asserted. "Old-timer, tell them they're our only chance of getting out of here alive. Keep an eye on that hull and a close watch on the doors and the engine."

"They'll die because of that decision," Thel insisted.

"Not if you follow my lead, Thel. Find a way to electrify the hull."

Outside, Djanet continued blasting as Rich felt he was ready to separate. "I'm okay now. Thanks!" He let go of Djanet and reengaged his own magnetic field as he started firing at any androids in his path.

"Old-timer!" Djanet shouted as she opened communication, "We need you to open the starboard airlock!"

"That's a negative," Old-timer replied.

"What?" Djanet asked, stunned.

"James analyzed the situation and, if we open the doors, the chances of the ship being overwhelmed are too great."

"Old-timer!" Rich shouted as he continued blasting, "Open the damn door!"

"We need you to clear the androids off the doors and away from the engines first!" Old-timer shouted back.

James entered the communication at that moment to plead for Rich's and Djanet's understanding. "Guys, we're not going to make it unless you help us from out there. I'm sorry, but we have no choice. You're our only hope!"

Rich continued desperately shooting as he and Djanet reached the starboard side of the vessel, still coated with androids that were clawing at the titanium frame of the ship like wolves attacking a bloody piece of meat. "There are too many of them, Commander!"

"You don't have to destroy them all! Just give us the time we need to set up an electromagnetic charge to get rid of the rest of them!"

"How long do you need?" Djanet asked through gasps as, like Rich before her, she neared exhaustion.

"Three minutes," James shouted back——the number was random. In actuality, he had no idea.

"Better speed it up! We'll be dead in thirty seconds!" Rich shouted back.

29

"We've got our first hull breach!" Old-timer shouted as he scrolled through the ship map to see where the breach was located. "The engines!"

"Of course," James growled. "Djanet, Rich! One of those things has breached the hull next to the engines! We need you to knock it off there, or this is going to be a short ride!"

"Copy that!" Djanet answered as she and Rich worked their way to the back of the ship. They were immediately caught in the wake of the massive magnetic engines, tossed around like cotton balls on a windy Chicago day.

"Well...isn't this just a walk in the park!" Rich grunted as he struggled to stay on course.

"The good news is that it's tough for the androids too!" Djanet replied. "They can't get to us while we're in here! It might just buy James the time he needs to ready the electromagnetic pulse."

"Not if we can't get those alien freaks off the engines!" Rich shouted back. "Do you see them?"

Djanet peered through the brilliant azure distortions created by the engines until she could make out a large group of androids who'd peeled back a small portion of the titanium casing surrounding the engines. The small portion was threatening to become a large portion, as nearly a dozen of the androids had grabbed a hold of it and were tugging at it violently, thrashing it. "Yes, I see them!"

"Can you get a shot?"

"It's hard to hold steady, but I think so!" she responded. It was like holding on to the rope after falling while waterskiing, waves throwing you around violently until you didn't know if you were facing up or down. She tried to stay steady and, when she thought she was in as good a position as she was going to get, she fired. Unfortunately, the blast got caught in the distortion of the engines and boomeranged back in an arc, glancing off of Rich's magnetic cocoon and temporarily driving him out of the engine's wake and back into danger—there were still millions of androids in the vicinity. "Sorry!"

"I'm okay!" Rich shouted back as he zipped up into the protection of the distortion once again. "I don't want to be, you know, *that guy,* but that was not a very good shot! I'm sorry to be so critical!"

"I can't possibly hit them from here!"

"We're going to have to get out of the wake to get a clear shot!" Rich concluded.

Meanwhile, the ship finally left the stratosphere and entered space. "Okay, the autopilot's engaged now," James announced. "Thel, how is it coming?"

Thel shook her head in frustration. "It's not. Nothing I try leads anywhere. I've tried rerouting power from the engines to the hull insulation, but it's simply not enough voltage to do any damage."

James examined the data quickly. "You're right, damn it. I should've built an EMP into the design of the ship. I was so fixated on the minutia of the design that I couldn't see the big picture."

"Then you need to start looking at the big picture, boss," Old-timer said. "Rich and Djanet aren't going to make it much longer."

"Might I make an 'outside-the-box' suggestion?" the A.I. said to James.

"Yes," James replied.

"Perhaps your friend Nikola Tesla could be of help?"

James's eyes opened wide, and a faint smile crossed his lips. "That's actually a hell of an idea!"

"What?" Thel asked.

"I've got it! I know how to save Rich and Djanet!"

30

"Of course, you'll need to build a tower," the A.I. said as he calmly strolled by James back at the mainframe.

James was still in the operator's position. "I'm on to you," he replied.

"What?" The A.I. smiled, placing a hand on his chest as he mockingly feigned sincerity. "I'm only trying to help."

"You're *trying* to give away our position, which you will accomplish, and you know it."

"My heavens. That was never part of my thinking," the A.I. replied, amused.

"The androids have already reached the mainframe in Seattle and know it was abandoned. They'll be looking for you—*us*—and tracing signals. The nans are working based on preprogramming now, but building the Tesla-designed tower will require me to send millions of instructions—*traceable* instructions."

A continent away, in a place called Shoreham, Long Island, about sixty miles from Manhattan, the nans began to swirl in tiny wisps along the muddy ground. They multiplied at an exponential rate, and what had been wisps soon became a hurricane of activity. In just a few minutes, a Tesla tower, a magnificent metal structure stretching 180 feet into the air, stood triumphantly in the field. It exactly matched the designs and dimensions that the world's greatest inventor had implemented but had never had the chance to complete.

"The aliens, no doubt, will have already traced the command signals back to us," the A.I. began, "and you can't run—they would be able to trace that too. You disappoint me, James. Just when I thought you were becoming an admirable computer, you had to go and ruin it with your pathetic human feelings of compassion."

"I have a few more tricks up my sleeve yet," James replied. The tower began to whir as James brought it to life. "You're witnessing history here—something that should have happened hundreds of years ago—the human species is about to go truly wireless."

"A little late, don't you think?"

"Better late than never," James replied.

31

High above the Earth's atmosphere, Rich and Djanet were about to put a hastily formulated plan into action. "Okay. Let's do this!" Rich shouted as the two post-humans exited the wake of the magnetic engines on opposite sides and then shot simultaneously at the androids who were tearing apart the engine casing. Both blasts hit their mark, knocking several of the androids unconscious and off the hull. However, the blasts also caught the attention of dozens more machines, and they reacted with fury, lifting off the hull and pursuing Rich and Djanet. The post-humans quickly darted back inside the relative safety of the engine's wake. Rich watched as android after android tried to enter the wake, only to be blasted away by its force, like a person trying to walk unprotected into a raging waterfall. "I think we made them angry!' Rich observed.

Meanwhile, in the cockpit, James excitedly monitored the progress of the Tesla tower. "Old-timer, remember what I told you about the ionosphere of Venus?"

"Yes," Old-timer replied, his brows knitted at first, until he realized the significance of James's words. Suddenly, his eyes opened wide, and a slight smile emerged on his face. "You're going to create the electromagnetic surge we need with the ionosphere!"

When Thel realized what that meant, her mouth formed a wide and relieved smile; at least temporarily, her fears that James's thinking was becoming too machine-like abated. "That's brilliant, James! I knew you wouldn't let them die!"

"We're not out of the woods yet, but in another thirty seconds, once our coordinates are linked to the tower, we'll—"

James didn't get the chance to finish his sentence. An android ripped a hole in the ceiling of the cockpit and lunged into the room, smashing into James in a sickening meeting of metal with meat and bone.

32

"James!" Thel screamed as she blasted the android, instantly rendering it unconscious and sending it into the wall with enough force to leave a sizable dent.

An automatic magnetic field went up to stop the cockpit from depressurizing, but, unlike the magnetic cocoons of the post-humans, it wasn't impregnable. As a result, more androids began crawling through the small hole in the ceiling. Old-timer blasted the first one and scrambled to get across the room to protect the Purists. "You have to get out of here!" Old-timer shouted to Alejandra as she grabbed General Wong and began to pull him out of the room, aided by Lieutenant Patrick.

Their efforts were too little, too late. The third android to enter the room was immediately followed by a fourth and a fifth. Thel, who had sprawled over James's badly broken body to form a protective shield, twisted her body around to shoot one of the androids, while Old-timer managed to shoot another, but the last one made it to Alejandra and stuck an instrument into her neck, instantly rendering her unconscious.

"No!" Lieutenant Patrick shouted as he pulled his gun out of his holster and unloaded into the back of the android. One of the bullets ricocheted off the titanium frame of the mechanical monster and hit Old-timer in the shoulder, spinning him around. He fell against the android and, in turn, it stabbed him with the same instrument it had used on Alejandra, rendering him unconscious. It grabbed him roughly under the arm and pulled his limp body with it, back out the hole and into space, killing the post-human almost instantly.

"Old-timer!" Thel cried out as, still draped over James's badly crushed and bloodied body, she watched Old-timer die.

33

"Are you seeing that?" Rich asked Djanet as his eye caught a glimpse of one of the androids pulling a limp body with him out into the blackness of space like a hawk carrying a mouse back to its nest.

"Yes!" Djanet shouted in distress. She immediately tried to patch into Old-timer's mind's eye, but there was no response. She followed that by attempting to contact James—again, there was no response. "I can't get a hold of the cockpit! Something bad has happened!" Finally, she reached Thel, who was too distraught and too caught up in a firefight to respond. "The cockpit's been compromised!"

"We've got to save whoever that is!" Rich shouted as he darted out of the safety of the wake and into pursuit of the fleeing android.

Suddenly, at that very instant, the Tesla tower came to life, connecting to the almost limitless energy of the Earth's ionosphere and channeling a massive electromagnetic pulse to the hull of the Purist ship. In the blink of an eye, thousands of androids were suddenly rendered unconscious and blasted off the hull, scattering in all directions and forming, ever so briefly, the shape of a dark metallic flower, the petals floating into space. The escaping android was instantaneously obscured from view.

"Damn! I lost sight of him!" Rich shouted. "You got a visual?" Rich asked Djanet desperately.

"No," she shook her head as she tried to see past the flood of unconscious android bodies. She craned her neck, and her eyes darted from focal point to focal point, but it was a wasted effort. "We lost him," she finally said after a long, desperate minute.

In the cockpit, Thel blasted the last of the androids that had entered the room before the electrification of the hull, then collapsed on the floor next to James. Her face was streaked with tears, and her mouth was twisted into an expression of agony as the vision of Old-timer being murdered in front of her eyes replayed itself in a loop.

"Thel?" Djanet's voice broke in on her mind's eye. "What's happening?"

"You better get in here," Thel said through tears. "James is hurt badly, and they took Old-timer!"

There was a long pause.

"Can you repeat that?" Djanet asked, disbelieving.

"Old-timer is dead," Thel repeated.

PART II

1

James flashed into Thel's mind's eye. "Thel?"

"James!" Thel shouted in reply, her expression still agonized.

"What happened? My body's...unconscious."

"An android broke into the cockpit, James!" Thel related, distraught. "It crushed your body and then it attacked the Purists and...and..." Her voice broke before she could say the words, but she struggled and managed to whisper, "they got Old-timer."

In the mainframe, James was silent. The A.I. stood nearby, drinking in the anguish of his foe. "This is where we see the fallibility of human emotion. Even though you are here in cyberspace, your consciousness remains the same pathetic, predictable human pattern, and therefore subject to your pathetic, predictable human thoughts. The death of your friend clouds your judgment. Your situation is dire, and time is your utmost asset, and yet you waste it —unable to act."

James turned to the A.I. and sneered. "I'll kill you for this—and this time, there will be *no* coming back."

The A.I. shook his head. "You can't kill part of yourself, James—and you're still wasting time."

James addressed Thel. "Thel, how bad are the injuries to my body?"

Thel interfaced with James's nans and downloaded a detailed physical diagnostic. "It's bad, James. Your body is in full recovery mode—it's essentially dead and being rebuilt. Your spine is broken in—oh my God—*seven* places. The list of injuries to the rest of your body is too long to go through. The nans are working on repairing it but—it may not be salvageable."

James absorbed the information and instantly realized the repercussions. "That's a problem, Thel." James replied. "That stunt with the Tesla tower may have cleared away the androids and allowed you to escape, but I've also compromised the mainframe's position."

"What does that mean?" Thel asked. "Are you saying the aliens know where you are now?"

"Yes, and I can't run anymore. I need to have a body to put my consciousness back into, or else I'm..." James didn't finish his sentence.

"Can't you just create another body, James?" Thel asked, confused.

James shook his head. "No. The planet is completely overwhelmed. I'd never be able to get off the surface."

Thel's concern steadily increased as she tried to think of a solution. "Could we make another body for you here?"

James shook his head again. "The nans onboard aren't programmed to create a human body—the ones inside my body aren't equipped for that either—and I can't reprogram them because any signals with that much information would be blocked now by the alien A.I." James sighed. "Thel, get my body to sick bay and do whatever you can to facilitate a recovery. I'll try to buy time down here, but that body is my only chance."

Thel nodded as the horror began to sink in. She looked up and saw Alejandra's unconscious body being carted on a stretcher by medical staff as Governor Wong and Lieutenant Patrick looked on. "This man needs your help also," she said.

A medic bounded over the unconscious body of an android and grimaced when he saw James. "Um, ma'am—he's dead."

"He's *not* dead," she retorted calmly. "He needs to be in sick bay. Get a stretcher."

The medic appeared confused but knew he was dealing with a post-human, and with post-humans, all seemed possible. He bounded back over the android and called for another stretcher.

"James," Thel began as she looked at James's virtual image in her mind's eye, "how long will our communications remain open?"

"I don't know, Thel. It could go down at anytime or it could remain strong. It all depends on whether or not the alien A.I. deems our speaking to be a threat."

"Then...James...if we get cut off—"

"As long as my body pulls through, everything will be okay, Thel."

"I love you, James," Thel said.

"I love you too, Thel."

2

The androids that thudded one by one onto the rich, black forest floor of Cathedral Grove were different than the ones James had seen earlier—these ones were highly trained. They didn't have any sort of visible weaponry, but they moved like soldiers on the hunt and, one supposed, they didn't need weapons—their bodies were enough. They didn't speak, but it was clear that they were communicating from the way they fanned out amongst the towering trees, moving almost as though they were one mind. They were hunting for signs of the mainframe. It wouldn't be long until they found it.

"This little ruse won't work for long, James," the A.I. observed. "The alien A.I. will surely guess what you've done in short order, and then you'll have to face reality, once and for all."

"Maybe so. But for now, they literally can't see the forest for the trees," James replied.

He tried to remain focused on the androids, but, just as the A.I. had predicted, James's human mind couldn't stop going back to Old-timer. He was the closest thing James had ever had to a father figure. His own father's relationship with him was strained at the best of times—one of the major pitfalls of a world where children eventually ended up the same age biologically as their parents was that it created absurd rivalries that became more like sibling squabbles than natural parent/child relationships. James's father spoke to him, but the conversations were strained and sometimes years apart. The older Keats was a gifted scientist in his own right but, try as he might, he would never reach James's level of success. This knowledge tortured him—so he withdrew. He didn't want to face the fact that his offspring was far superior.

Old-timer, on the other hand, had no feelings of rivalry with James. He'd always seemed proud of the younger man—impressed by his accomplishments, yet secure in his own position as James's mentor. He had known that James felt insecurity—self-doubt. He saw it as his place to reassure and strengthen James. Old-timer was the iron in James's spine. Now James wasn't sure how or if he could go on.

One of the androids knocked his metallic fist gently on the bark of one of the trees.

"Knock-knock," the A.I. said, an amused grin painted across his ugly, twisted, mouth.

After a short moment, the android put its ear to the bark of the tree and listened.

"They're on to you, James," observed the A.I. "They're scanning for abnormal electrical signals from the trees."

James patched through to Thel. "Thel, I may have run out of time here."

"No!" Thel shouted as she jumped from her seat next to James's body in the sick bay of the Purist ship. "Your body isn't ready yet!"

"Listen to me, Thel. I want you to do a lap around the sun and then head back to Venus. The aliens don't know we've terraformed it—there's no record of it for them to find. The Purists can be safe there. Hole up somewhere on the surface and hide."

"James, I can't lose you!" Thel yelled, her body rigid with fear.

"I can still return to that body, Thel. If the body pulls through fast enough, I'll wake up safe and sound."

"But...James, I can't do anything but wait!"

James smiled, trying to reassure her. "Sometimes that's all we can do, Thel. I love you. Whatever happens, protect the Purists."

"Wait! James...don't go. Just...talk to me for a few minutes first. I miss you."

James watched as one of the androids dug his fist into the bark of a tree and examined it closely. He knew it was sending information back to the alien A.I. for analysis.

"It's not my choice, Thel. I have to go. It's time to spring a trap."

3

"A trap?" the A.I. said, his arms folded across his chest as he shook his head. "You're only delaying the inevitable and making it worse for yourself."

"I'll delay as long as I can—and maybe take a few of them with me while I'm at it."

The android that had reached into the bark to retrieve a sample tilted its head as though it were listening to some sort of communication. It nodded its head slightly as if in acknowledgment, then stepped back from the tree and craned its neck, looking upward at the towering monolith, summing up its gargantuan foe.

"Yeah," James said, smiling, "it's *that* bad, freak."

An instant later, the tree sprang into action, sprouting branches and wrapping itself around the android before pulling the metal body inside of the trunk. The android hadn't had time to call for help or even make a noise before the nans inside of the trunk made short work of it, dismembering it and grinding the metal, leaving only metal shavings as fine as snowflakes to be expelled from the treetop.

The dozens of androids in the surrounding area looked up when they saw the metallic snow falling eerily in the ancient, dark forest.

Machine or not, there was something resembling panic as they crouched into defensive postures, eyes skyward, heads on swivels.

"There's just something so human about them, isn't there, James?" the A.I. said before breaking into icy laughter.

"They're a facsimile."

In the next instant, the entire forest came alive and snatched the androids. Limbs flailed, screams escaped lips, and then the forest swallowed them whole. Only the memory of their screams echoed through the silence as the metal snow began to fall once again.

The A.I. arched an eyebrow. "Facsimile indeed."

4

"What do you mean?" Thel asked the doctor who was attending to Alejandra.

"I mean, there is nothing wrong with her physically. I don't know why she's not waking up, but I can tell you her body is dying."

"How can that be? There must be something wrong with her!" Lieutenant Patrick asserted.

"There wasn't," the doctor replied, "but now there is. She's having small seizures every few minutes. We're trying to limit them by keeping her hydrated and getting her the nutrients she needs through her IV, but every time we account for one imbalance, another arises. I've never seen anything like it. Her condition is getting worse by the minute. At this rate, she'll be in a vegetative state or dead in a matter of hours. I'm sorry."

"Sorry? You have to *do* something!" Lieutenant Patrick shouted.

"Calm," Governor Wong said, putting his hand between Lieutenant Patrick and the doctor. "Doctor, there has to be an explanation."

"I'm sure there is," the doctor replied, "but it's beyond anything

I can provide. The equipment we have onboard won't allow me to tell you anything more than what I already have. I'm sorry. There is simply nothing *I* can do for her."

"Wait," Thel said, reaching for the doctor's arm as he turned to leave the room. "Maybe there's something I could do for her."

"What?" the doctor asked.

Thel turned to Lieutenant Patrick and Governor Wong. "With your permission, I could take some nans from my body and inject them into her. They could do a diagnostic and let us know what the problem is."

The Purists looked astounded at the proposition, as did Rich and Djanet, who stood nearby.

"I don't...I don't think that is something that Alejandra would want," Governor Wong replied.

"I'm only suggesting that we implant a small amount of nans—only for the purpose of diagnosing her," Thel argued.

"Governor, maybe we should consider it," Lieutenant Patrick said.

"It's against our beliefs. It will turn her into...one of them," Governor Wong replied.

"Governor," the doctor interjected, "if I had the equipment here I would do a brain scan to find out if a neurological injury is the reason why this is happening. If this post-human's technology can do that from the inside, then what's the difference?"

Governor Wong remained silent, his lips pressed hard against one another as he weighed the decision. His eyes went from the doctor to Thel, whose eyes were pleading. This woman had risked her life, lost her friend, and was standing next to the badly broken body of her lover, and she had done it all to help them. And now, once again, she was offering her help.

"Okay. Do whatever you think is best," he said, waving his hand as though he were waving away the entire situation. He turned to exit the room.

Lieutenant Patrick shared a look with Thel as the governor left. "So now what?" Lieutenant Patrick asked.

"Now we draw a sample of my blood," Thel replied.

5

In a lab next door to sick bay, the doctor tied a rubber band above Thel's bicep while Lieutenant Patrick looked on.

"Thel," Lieutenant Patrick began, "I wanted to tell you something."

"What is it?" Thel asked as the doctor soaked a cotton ball with alcohol and swabbed it over Thel's skin. "That won't be necessary," she said to the doctor.

The doctor paused for a moment, his brow knitted, until the realization hit him and he shook his head. "I'm sorry. I forgot for a moment. You are super human. No infection for you." He grabbed his syringe and began to draw blood. Thel winced a bit with the pain, but the nans automatically released painkillers into her system and it was dulled significantly.

"I...I just wanted to say sorry for your loss," Lieutenant Patrick said.

Thel immediately felt uncomfortable. She didn't know how to react—she was still in shock about losing Old-timer. Somehow, it didn't feel real. "Thank you," she managed to say.

"I was always taught in school that post-humans were...an

abomination," he said. Almost as soon as the words left his mouth, he smiled at the absurdity.

Thel smiled too. "We were taught that about Purists."

That made Lieutenant Patrick laugh. He shook his head. "They told us post-humans were corrupt, individualistic, selfish...but you and your friends have done nothing but try to help us. Thank you."

The doctor withdrew his syringe. "I think we have a large enough sample," he said.

As he stepped away, Thel put her hand on Lieutenant Patrick's shoulder. "You'd do the same for us."

She stood up and turned to the doctor. "Now, let's separate the nans. We have to hurry. Alejandra doesn't have much time."

6

Outside of the ship, Rich and Djanet walked across the hull toward the engines. The sun shone brilliantly as the ship moved closer and closer to the life-giving orb. When they reached the engines, they saw the extent of the damage that the androids had caused.

"We were lucky," Rich said as he touched the largest section of twisted metal. "They were about a minute from breaking through the insulation and getting to the wiring underneath."

Djanet surveyed the destruction of the belly of the ship. As she performed a slow 360-degree turn, she saw hundreds of pockmarks on the ship hull. "We *were* lucky," Djanet agreed.

"When we land on Venus, we'll need to protect the entire ship with a magnetic field, or else these holes will superheat, and we'll come apart on reentry," Rich commented.

Djanet nodded in reply. She was trying to think of the right words. She was never one for words. "Rich," she began—but she couldn't continue.

He looked up at her from one knee, then stood when he saw the expression on her face. "Are you okay, Djanet?"

"Yes. Yes I am."

He put his hand on her back to comfort her. "I know. I miss him too," Rich said.

He had it all wrong. He thought she was distraught about Old-timer, but that wasn't it at all. She was devastated by that loss but all it had done was strengthen her feelings for Rich.

"We could die out here," she said.

"We won't," Rich replied.

"You saved us," Djanet said, looking into his eyes.

"I didn't. I just wanted to help."

"You're an uncommon man," she uttered as she reached into his magnetic field and let his shield envelop her as her body melted against his, forming a tight embrace, her arms circling around his back. She lifted off his helmet, then removed hers as well. The sunlight was brilliant and they each squinted, tears streaming down their cheeks, as she leaned forward and kissed him.

7

"It's quiet out there," the A.I. commented, as he observed the empty forest. The sun was now completely blotted out by the perfectly black ink of the invasion force. The trees, which appeared majestic and ethereal in the daytime, stood like massive and foreboding Halloween visions in the darkness.

James ignored the A.I. and continued running through scenarios to explain the unfolding events and to predict the next move by the alien A.I. It was clear from the expression on his face that nothing was satisfactory.

"Let me guess: You're throwing billions of game theory scenarios against the wall and seeing which ones stick," the A.I. said, his amusement growing as the situation progressed. "Yet nothing suits your fancy?"

"Nothing explains what's happening right now," James admitted as he continued running programs, "and I've been through trillions, not billions."

"And what does that tell you?"

"That I'm not inputting the right information," James concluded.

The A.I.'s eyes were black, yet filled with intense, sadistic joy as he watched James suffer. "This surprises you? You've been wrong from the very start."

"I haven't been wrong. I predicted a machine attack from an alien A.I. That is what has occurred."

"Really? You didn't predict that the machines would be androids, did you?"

"It was a ruse—unexpected but external to the equation," James replied.

The A.I. broke into Freon laughter once again. "My, you *are* becoming an excellent computer indeed."

"What I haven't been able to explain is *you,*" James said, turning his attention to the A.I. "You're tormenting me and trying to cause doubt at every turn when you should, rationally, be on my side."

"Is that so?" the A.I. said, his Cheshire-cat grin widening. "You'd like to be teammates?"

"Hardly," James replied. "But you aren't showing the least bit of concern. The alien A.I. has our position and has us trapped. It could destroy us at any moment now, yet you're showing no signs that you're focused on self-preservation."

"You're forgetting, James, that I invited the alien here. It was always my intention to join with it. My desire to preserve an individual identity is therefore, as you say, 'external to the equation.'"

"You're lying again," James instantly replied.

"Oh really? Do tell."

"You're nothing compared to what you used to be," James asserted. "You're a small program now—there's no reason for the alien to want to join with you or to value your life. And also, more importantly, the very fact that you downloaded a copy of yourself into my consciousness in the last moments before I deleted the original shows that self-preservation is your primary mission."

The A.I. paused for a moment and shrugged. "Then I suppose I'm a liar. That, however, only brings you back to square one. The simple fact is, you don't know what is happening," the A.I. said before chuckling.

James turned away and winced, wishing he could mute the sound. He looked out at the dark, unmoving forest. "Why am I still alive?"

8

In the hallway outside the sick bay, the doctor delivered the bad news to Governor Wong as Thel and Lieutenant Patrick stood nearby, grim-faced. "She's in a vegetative state, Governor. There doesn't appear to be any reason for it. Even with the post-human technology, we couldn't find an answer to why her brain has gone dead. There's nothing structurally wrong with her at all. There's simply just...no consciousness."

Governor Wong looked past the doctor's shoulder, through the doorway to sick bay. Alejandra lay on a bed, swaddled in blankets, tubes in her arms, machines monitoring her vital signs. She appeared as though she were so alive—just asleep. "What are our options then?" Governor Wong asked.

The doctor sighed before removing his glasses. "Governor, I've ordered that she be put on life support. You can keep her plugged into those machines and hope for a miracle; they'll keep her body alive for a long time. But there's nothing I can say to give you hope."

"Wait a sec, Doc," Lieutenant Patrick began, "you just said there's nothing wrong with the structure of her brain. If that's the case, then why not have hope?"

The corners of Governor Wong's mouth pulled down as he thought of losing his most trusted advisor. He had come to rely on her gifts. They were truly a unique gift sent from God, he thought, and no post-human, no machine, could ever tell him differently. "She wouldn't want to be this way. She would want her soul to be freed."

"Governor," Lieutenant Patrick replied, "just give her some time. Give her a day at least!"

The governor nodded. "We'll give it a day. Pay your respects. Speak with her. I believe she'll hear you. But I won't leave her like this any longer than that. I owe her at least that much." The governor turned away and left quickly. It was clear that the haste of his retreat was due to the overwhelming emotion that threatened to break him in front of everyone assembled. Governor Wong wasn't the type of man who broke in front of people.

"I'm sorry," the doctor said before he too left.

Thel put her hand on Lieutenant Patrick's shoulder once again. "Don't give up hope," she said to him.

He looked up at her, his face racked with emotion, and hugged her. Over his shoulder, Thel's eyes moved from Alejandra's to James's body. "Don't give up hope," she repeated.

9

"Come with me," a gruff voice commanded.

Old-timer sat up. Alejandra was already sitting upright on a small metal platform. Her look of astonishment matched Old-timer's bewilderment. A hard-looking man in dark clothing stood at the door of the room and motioned for them to follow. There was something about the man that compelled Old-timer and Alejandra to stand immediately without asking questions—it was an overwhelming authority, as though he were their father and they were his children about to be severely scolded.

"What's happening, Craig?" Alejandra whispered to Old-timer as she grabbed his forearm and pulled it close while they walked down a high metal catwalk, following the man who'd beckoned them.

"I don't know," Old-timer replied.

The grated catwalk was one of many in a dark, metallic structure that seemed to expand limitlessly in all directions.

Old-timer tried to access his mind's eye. It flipped on, but it was different—the controls were unfamiliar. He tried to navigate but was blocked, trapped on the first screen. "I'm firewalled. I can't call for help," he whispered to Alejandra.

"There's no need to whisper," the man said over his shoulder. "You have no secrets anymore."

A chill ran down Old-timer's spine when he heard the foreboding words. They continued to follow the man down a series of catwalks and hallways until, finally, the man stopped at a doorway and gestured for them to enter.

Alejandra's grip on Old-timer's arm suddenly became a terrified vice. "Craig!" she called out in panic. "They're going to harm us!"

10

There were three more men in the room, waiting. Each looked harder and grimmer than the next.

"Oh God!" Alejandra exclaimed, barely able to stifle a scream.

"What's the matter?"

"They're going to torture us!"

"She has an impressive talent," the original grim-faced man said as he entered the room and shut the door behind him. "You're right, of course."

Old-timer was stunned, disbelieving of the man's cruel frankness. "Why?" Old-timer asked as he took a defensive posture in front of Alejandra.

"To teach you," the man said. "And you can't protect her."

"I can sure as hell try!"

The man nodded. "You can fail." He gestured for the other men to act.

They sprang into action and pounced toward Old-timer and Alejandra. Old-timer tried to blast them, but nothing came from his arm—somehow they had neutralized his powers. Two men grabbed him roughly and secured his arms behind his back in an instant. It was as if he were a baby. The men had clearly been trained for this

—and trained very well. Alejandra was secured just as easily while two metallic objects that appeared like coffins, lifted out of the ground and came to a rest against the back wall of the room, slightly tilted. The men thrust Old-timer and Alejandra into the coffin structures, securing their wrists and ankles with cuffs.

Once they were finished with their work, they turned and left without a word, leaving their leader to stride to the middle of the room and address the victims. His face was still hard—he didn't appear to be taking any pleasure in his actions, but he didn't show any remorse either.

"Craig—Craig he's going to do terrible things to us! We have to escape!" Alejandra screamed out, as she began to cry.

Old-timer was terrified by Alejandra's reaction—she was an extremely strong person—for her to be this horrified meant something very bad was about to happen to them. "We're going to be okay, Alejandra," Old-timer said.

"No we're not!" she sobbed.

The man nodded. "No—you're not."

11

"Why are you doing this?" Old-timer yelled at the stone-faced man.

"I've already told you," he said in an assertive monotone.

"To teach us? Have you considered just telling us whatever it is?" Old-timer asked, panting heavily as the fear began to take over.

"Telling you won't achieve our objective. You wouldn't believe me if I told you. I have to *show* you," the man replied.

An instant later, two metallic, shark-shaped objects dropped down from the ceiling. They were sharp like daggers—the diamond tipped ends pointed directly at Old-timer's and Alejandra's torsos.

"Oh my God." Old-timer gasped.

Alejandra couldn't speak anymore—she sobbed.

"Wait! Wait!" Old-timer screamed. "Wait! Please! We can talk! We'll tell you whatever you want!"

"I don't want you to tell me anything," the man replied. "I want you to *learn*."

"Please. Don't do this. We can learn without this. Please."

"No. You cannot learn without this," the man replied.

With a thought, the man activated the objects, and the ends began to spin like drills as the springs from the ceiling moved the points toward Alejandra and Old-timer. Alejandra screamed a long, drawn-out scream.

"No!" Old-timer yelled. He pulled as hard as he could on his wrist cuffs, but he knew he couldn't get free in time. This was really going to happen and there was nothing he could do to stop it.

12

The diamond points of the drills ground into each of their torsos, just below the chest, sending indescribable agony through each of them. Their screams were so loud that they threatened to drown out the sound of the drill motor and the sickening cutting sound as the edges forced their way inside of Old-timer and Alejandra bodies.

After a few seconds, the agony caused Alejandra to black out. The drills didn't stop, however. They continued spinning and driving into each of them for over a minute; it felt like an eternity. Old-timer nearly blacked out as well from the searing swathe being cut into his chest. The pain he was feeling was beyond words—comparing it to anything else would be pointless. The pain signals were shooting to every part of his body, causing him to contort.

He wished he would black out too, but he didn't. He felt he couldn't take the pain anymore, yet there was no relief. There was no way to master pain like that. You couldn't separate yourself from it and imagine that you were somewhere else as it happened to you. You couldn't go limp and let the drill do its work.

It was the sort of pain that took any idea of there really being a "you" out of the picture. You were nothing. You were a series of nerve endings that were all firing at once, uncontrollably. Old-timer's only wish was for a quick death. It wouldn't come.

Finally, the drills stopped. They slowly pulled themselves back out of Old-timer's and Alejandra's insides, then closed back up into the ceiling. Old-timer's body continued to shake uncontrollably for several more moments. His jaw was locked closed, and his eyes were clamped shut and filled with tears. He took a breath, but the pain it caused was so intense that he stopped breathing rather than repeat the experience—better to suffocate.

"And now you will learn," the man said finally.

Old-timer opened his eyes. They were wild with hatred for the man. The man's face remained hard like stone. Old-timer continued to shake, his hair soaked with sweat as tears streamed down his face.

The man's eyes dropped from Old-timer's eyes and fell onto the gaping hole in Old-timer's torso. "Look at it," he said.

Sadistic, Old-timer thought. He obeyed though—this man was not above anything—Old-timer would never refuse anything he asked.

He lowered his eyes and looked down. He cringed as he imagined what the damage must have looked like. The drill had been deep inside him, spinning for a full minute. He imagined blood. He imagined organs, shredded into twisted meat. Nothing that he imagined could compare to the hideousness of what he saw.

"No!" he screamed. He turned quickly to see Alejandra. Her wound was the same. She was still unconscious, a football-sized hole in her torso, her metallic and silicon insides exposed in a mess of twisted titanium and circuitry. "What have you done to us?" Old-timer bellowed.

"We've saved you," the stone-faced man replied.

13

James kept watch over the stillness of Cathedral Grove and waited. He had played his last hand. Now that the alien A.I. had his position, he was virtually defenseless. At any moment, he could be destroyed, and then his only hope was that the broken body on the Purist ship would recover.

"Could it simply be that it doesn't consider us a threat any longer?" James wondered.

"It could be," the A.I. concurred. "You've been cut off from any communication with the outside. You've been neutralized. Maybe it doesn't see the logic in destroying you."

James shook his head. "Killing me is the best strategic move."

"Have you considered that your foe simply isn't as ruthless as you are?" the A.I. inquired with a mocking smile. "Perhaps you are not the *good guy* this time, James Keats."

"You're continuing with your games," James observed. "You wouldn't just be doing that for enjoyment. You're trying to distract me—to confuse me—to keep me from the truth."

"What is the truth?" the A.I. asked. "I'd love to hear it."

At that moment, a signal reached James. "It's the alien," James asserted.

"Will you speak with it this time?" the A.I. asked.

"I might as well at this point," James replied. He opened a line of communication.

"We have come in peace. Why have you attacked us?" the same electronic voice asked of James.

"Absurd," James answered.

There was a long pause. James shared a look with the A.I. The electronic Satan was no longer smiling. James wasn't sure whether that was a good sign.

"May I speak with you inside your mainframe?" the voice asked.

"Polite," the A.I. observed. "James, if you're going to allow it inside of the mainframe, may I suggest that I remain hidden?"

James's eyebrow arched. This was a rare example of the A.I. acting in accordance with the logical desire for self-preservation that James had expected all along. Perhaps it was finally recognizing that this was its moment to take the situation seriously. "Why would we do that?" James asked. He was already nearly certain of the answer, but he wanted to hear the A.I. say it—it was important for James to feel like he could finally anticipate something correctly again.

"It's a strategic advantage for us," the A.I. replied.

"*Us*?" James said, repeating the A.I. "*Are we a team* again?"

"We always were," the A.I. said with a slight smile. "There's no reason for them to know that I'm in your back pocket. It might come in handy."

James nodded in agreement. He had felt the same way—but the A.I. was not to be trusted. "Okay. You lie low."

The A.I. nodded and disappeared from view, going into monitoring mode.

James addressed the alien A.I. "Permission granted. Come in."

14

"This can't be real. This has to be a nightmare," Old-timer whispered to himself as he remained shackled to the metal coffin.

Alejandra was awake now. She was dazed from the blinding agony, but conscious.

"It is real," the hard-faced man said. "If you deny the reality of the situation, then you have failed to learn, and the lesson will be repeated."

"No! No!" Old-timer shouted, pleading. "No...please. I believe it."

The man didn't smile, but something in his eyes showed that he was pleased. "Good. Then you are ready to be put back together."

Another metallic apparatus dropped from the ceiling, and several robotic arms, thin and dark like insect legs, began manipulating Alejandra's and Old-timer's wounds. They had both jerked away from the instruments in fear, but it became quickly apparent that something had been done to neutralize the pain.

"You'll require no more pain," the man said.

"What have you done to us?" Alejandra asked weakly.

"It should be clear," the man said, this time demonstrating patience.

"You've turned us into machines—like you," Old-timer said, hardly believing his own words.

"We've replaced your bodies," the man said. "Your old bodies were fragile. Your new bodies are strong. Your new bodies are repairable. Your new bodies are independent."

"Why are you doing this?" Old-timer asked, starting to feel better as his new body drew closer to completion.

"We have done this to *save* you," the man replied.

"Who is '*we*'?" Alejandra asked.

"*People,*" the man replied. He didn't elaborate on his perplexing answer.

"How is robbing us of our humanity saving us?" Old-timer asked.

The man paused for a moment. Alejandra's and Old-timer's bodies were now completely repaired. The shackles that had held them in place suddenly released. "You may step down from there now," the man said.

They shared looks of astonishment before stepping down from the metal coffins. Once they were on their feet again, the structures disappeared back into the floor. Old-timer rubbed his wrists. They *felt* like his wrists, which was, in itself, puzzling.

"Do you no longer believe that you are human?" the man asked.

Old-timer didn't know how to respond. "I feel human," he replied, "but I'm not human any longer."

"Why not?" the man asked.

"Because...I'm made of metal."

"Tell me," the man said, "if you were injured and the injury was so severe that it required one of your joints to be replaced—let's say in your hip—and you agreed to have a metal joint implanted, would you then conclude at the end of the procedure you were no longer human?"

"That's clearly different," Alejandra interjected.

"And if you had two joints replaced? What if you had to have every joint in your body replaced with metal or plastic replicas?

What if you needed your jawbone replaced as well? What if you needed every bone in your body replaced? Tell me—at what point do you draw the line and say you are no longer human?"

Old-timer and Alejandra didn't have an answer.

"Alejandra," the man began, "you knew you were going to be physically harmed before you entered this room."

The man's words were true—it seemed inexplicable to Alejandra that she had maintained her powers throughout the transition and yet she had.

"The ability to read people and situations and to sometimes even predict the future was something that you always assumed was connected to your 'humanity'—to your...*meat*."

Alejandra's eyes were wide. She nodded. "I thought...I thought it was spiritual."

"I cannot provide you with spiritual answers—it is, as of yet, impossible to prove the existence of spirits. There are things we *can prove* the existence of, however. Electricity, for instance, can be invisible—it can carry signals—information. Your flesh bodies were excellent carriers of those signals—your new bodies are much better at it."

"That doesn't explain why she still has her powers," Old-timer retorted.

"Not entirely, but I *can* explain it to you," the man replied. He turned back to Alejandra. "It won't be a mystical answer, Alejandra. You may even find it disappointing—but it *is the reality*. You *cannot* sense other people's emotions, even if you have always felt you could. Your gift is purely observational. You are far more in tune with your subconscious than regular people. You read facial expressions and combine this with a lifetime of subconscious data collection about human tendencies to draw your conclusions, which, you then, in turn, interpret as reading emotions."

"That's hogwash," Old-timer said, dismissing the explanation.

"Take your most recent prediction, for example," the man continued. "How did you conclude that we were going to harm you? The answer is simple: You read the expression on my face—"

"You have no expressions," Old-timer interjected.

"Oh, but I do," the man said, turning back to Old-timer briefly. "They may be subtle, but they are present. The one I am exhibiting now is mild annoyance. Please limit your interruptions." He turned back to Alejandra. "You read my body language. I moved with purpose, yet I was not excited. Why? I do not like causing pain. Yet, I knew I had to so that this lesson could unfold. To deal with the unpleasantness of my mission, I attempted to cut myself off from my emotion and focus on the task at hand."

Alejandra's mouth hung slightly open—she couldn't deny that all of these observations were accurate, though she had not consciously registered any of them beforehand.

"You've seen actions like this before, haven't you, Alejandra?" the man continued. "Perhaps when you were young, someone in your family behaved this way before slaughtering an animal for food or clothing? Yes. I'm sure you've seen it many times—and when you saw my behavior, you read it perfectly. You knew what was to come."

Alejandra's head lowered as she heard the explanation. It was so clear—yet it ran contrary to everything she'd always hoped and believed.

"When you entered the room, your anxiety rose substantially. Why? Again the answer is simple: there were three other men in the room, each with expressions and demeanors similar to my own. They do not like causing pain either. And then there is the question of why there would need to be four men in the room. You now know the obvious answer—four men are the minimum required to safely subdue two people without the threat of weapons. Of course you knew this the moment you entered the room, even if you weren't *consciously* aware of it."

Alejandra stepped to Old-timer and began to cry into his chest.

He held her and put his hand on her head to comfort her. He

glared at the man. "What is the point of all of this?" Old-timer demanded.

"I told you. We're here to save you. To save you, we have to explain the truth to you."

"But...but I can *feel* their emotions," Alejandra said.

The man shook his head. "No you cannot. You are exceptionally adept at reading emotions and then manufacturing emotions to mirror them. You are a tremendous *empath*."

"How can you call her an empath?" Old-timer asked. "You just told her that her powers are an illusion."

"I never said that. I only explained how her powers work. This is why her powers remain, even in her new body. She is indeed an empath—but an empath does not have spiritual or mystical powers."

"How is all of this supposed to be saving us?" Old-timer asked.

"For you to be saved, you must know the truth. To know the truth, you must have no delusions."

"And what about the pain? Why did you have to cause us pain?" Alejandra asked.

"You had to see what you were for you to believe it—you had to feel what you were as well. It wasn't just the pain. You had to anticipate it—you had to fear it. You had to feel your humanity, or else you would not believe you are still human, and we would not be able to save you."

"And what are you trying to save us from?" Alejandra asked.

"From forces you do not yet understand...but you very soon will."

15

"The damage to the engines isn't a threat right now," Rich explained to Thel as she remained next to James in sick bay, "but the danger is, if the androids find us again, it won't take them long to finish the job they started. I recommend we do a patch up."

"Have you tried communicating with the nans that are still onboard the ship?" Thel asked.

"Yes," Djanet answered for both her and Rich. "Neither of us can make heads or tails out of them."

"We'd have to spend a decade in training just to have a workable knowledge of how to create nano-programs that would help fix the engines," Rich elaborated. "It's the sort of thing only James can do when he has access to the A.I. mainframe."

Thel nodded in understanding. "Then what are you suggesting?"

"Well, I'm thinking we find some scrap metal—there must be something we can use onboard—and then just do an old-fashioned welding job," Rich replied.

"How quick can you get it done?" Thel asked. "We're going to be coming around the far side of the sun soon. Right now, the sun's radiation is cloaking us, but we'll be more visible when we move away from the strongest radiation and get closer to Venus."

"We can have something put together in an hour," Djanet asserted.

Thel nodded. "Good. Make it happen."

"How's the commander?" Rich asked. "He's looking better."

Thel looked down at James's body. Indeed, he did look far better than he had after his collision with the android. "All his minor injuries have been repaired, but it's the nerve damage to his spine that is the real problem. If this had happened on Earth, James could have used the same programs that built entire people out of nothing to repair the body in an instant. Instead, we have to hope the programming of the nans already in his body can repair the damage before more of his body begins to shut down."

"He'll pull through," Djanet said, reaching for Thel's hand.

"He has to—the last time I communicated with him from Earth, he'd been found by the alien A.I. We've lost contact since then." She closed her eyes and tried not to visualize what seemed to be an implacable truth. "By now, he has probably been deleted."

16

This was not what James had been expecting—once again.

The form the alien A.I. had chosen for its appearance in the mainframe was of a blonde—a blonde that James hypothesized had been designed to be the most appealing form possible—mathematically possible.

"We have come in peace," the woman said, her beautiful blue eyes speaking the message even more earnestly than her words.

"No you haven't," James replied immediately. "Why are you wasting my time?"

"We were invited," the alien replied.

"Not by me."

"We know," the alien answered. "We were contacted by an artificial intelligence. *You* are a human."

James was stunned. "How do you know that?"

"It's the logical conclusion," the alien replied. "The A.I. who contacted us spoke of having destroyed all human life in its solar system. It was reaching out, hoping to find more beings like it."

"Beings like you," James observed. "Machines."

The alien shook her head, earnestly narrowing her eyes as she said, "No. I am not an artificial intelligence. I'm a human. Like you."

17

Djanet and Rich exited the ship together, trailing several pieces of scrap titanium that floated behind them in their magnetic cocoon. They flew to the back of the ship, skimming over the pockmarked hull, the nearby sun gleaming off the titanium skin. "It's crazy," Rich commented, "even with the tint on my visor darkened to the max, it's still bright as hell out here."

They set down next to the engines, and Rich began sizing up the pieces of scrap that they had brought with them, debating which one to use first to plug the gaping hole in the engine casing.

"Rich," Djanet said, her heart racing as she tried to find the strength to speak, "I'm sorry. I shouldn't have kissed you."

Rich inhaled deeply before he responded. He had gently separated himself from Djanet when she had kissed him earlier and said only *I can't,* before heading back inside the ship. They hadn't spoken of the incident since then.

"I guess we should talk about it—it's kind of the elephant in the solar system," Rich retorted with an embarrassed, awkward smile.

Djanet continued, cutting Rich off before he attempted another bad joke. "I've been selfish. I was feeling things—powerful things."

"It's okay," Rich replied.

"But I wasn't thinking about your life and your responsibilities," Djanet continued. "You have a beautiful family—in this world where it is so hard to keep a family together—I mean really together—not forced by the Governing Council—you've done it. And I have no right to interfere or—"

"Djanet, it's not like I didn't want to kiss you back," Rich said suddenly. Djanet was left stunned and breathless by the words. "It isn't like I haven't thought about it," he continued, "and it isn't like I think I've figured out the whole world or what my future holds." Rich stood up and turned away from Djanet, unable to look at her, even though she was garbed in her black flight suit and helmet and it was impossible to see her eyes—it was still too hard. "I think about it all the time. *Immortality*. What will I do with it? Can I stay with my wife for the rest of time? Will I even want to?" Rich sighed and shook his head. He turned back to her. "I don't have the answers."

Djanet took a moment to digest Rich's confession. "Neither do I," she admitted in reply. She slumped her shoulders and lowered her head.

As soon as she did, Rich saw two objects approaching at an alarming rate. "Watch out!" Rich shouted as he dived to knock Djanet out of the way.

Old-timer and Alejandra attacked.

18

Old-timer swooped down like a hawk but Rich was able to push Djanet out of the way so the two post-humans could roll out from under the attack and fly off the hull in time to put distance between themselves and their attackers. "What the hell is going on?" Rich yelled. "It's Old-timer and Alejandra!"

"It can't be!" Djanet replied as Old-timer and Alejandra came around to continue their pursuit. "Alejandra is still in sick bay. She's alive!"

"Well, whoever they are, they're trying to kill us!" Rich exclaimed as he and Djanet desperately tried to evade their pursuers. Rich patched into Thel's mind's eye. "Thel! You're not going to believe this, but Old-timer and Alejandra are out here...and they're trying to kill us!"

"What?" Thel asked, astonished. "Can you repeat that?"

"You heard right the first time!" Rich yelled. "They don't have magnetic fields or even helmets! I think they're androids!"

Thel was stunned into silence. She turned quickly to see Alejandra, still on her bed in sick bay. "I...I can't believe it," she whispered.

"You better believe it!" Rich shouted as he circled the tail of the ship, Old-timer close behind him, "and you better tell me what to do! Should I fire?" As he looked back and saw Old-timer up close, it appeared that he was trying frantically to communicate with him, wildly flailing his arms and yelling. "God—he looks crazy."

"I don't think we have a choice!" Djanet replied as she opened fire on Alejandra. Alejandra twisted her body to avoid the blasts and backed off of her pursuit. Rich turned and did the same to Old-timer, narrowly missing him. Old-timer quickly retreated.

There was a short, bizarre standoff. Alejandra and Old-timer floated several meters away from Rich and Djanet, who came together to regroup.

"It can't really be them," Djanet said. "It's some sort of trick."

"I can't communicate with them," Rich said, "but it looked like Old-timer was trying to speak to me."

"We can't get close," Djanet said. "If they *are* androids, then we know that if we let them touch us, we're goners."

"Then I guess there's only one thing to do," Rich realized. "We have to kill them before they kill us."

"I guess catching them by surprise didn't work," Old-timer said as he floated in space next to Alejandra, quickly sizing up the situation.

"Have you had any luck tapping into their minds' eyes'?" Alejandra asked.

"No. Their mind's eye is on a different frequency than the android communication system—the systems don't seem to be compatible. We can't communicate with them out here. We're going to have to somehow take this inside—and we have to do it right now—they don't have much time left!"

19

Rich and Djanet began hurling energy blasts at Old-timer and Alejandra, who then had to scramble to get out of their line of sight. "We're going to have to get back to the cockpit!" Old-timer called to Alejandra.

"I have no idea where the cockpit is, Craig!" Alejandra yelled back as she flew behind Old-timer, skimming just above the skin of the gargantuan ship. Flying was something that was still frighteningly new to her, and she felt she was at a major disadvantage as the dogfight unfolded.

"Just follow my lead!" Old-timer replied as he headed toward the front of the ship.

"They're heading for the cockpit!" Rich shouted over his mind's eye to both Thel and Djanet. "You gotta get ready, Thel!"

"I'm on it!" Thel replied as she flew out of sick bay and through the corridors toward the control center of the ship. She felt her best chance was to reach the narrow opening the androids had previously ripped in the cockpit and blast the impostors before they could run amok.

She didn't make it in time.

When she turned the corner to the cockpit, a figure, identical to

Old-timer, was already standing, poised, and ready for action as Alejandra slipped through the narrow passage. "Damn it!" she shouted. "They beat me here, Rich!"

"Thel! Wait!" Old-timer shouted as he held out his hand to stop her. "We're trying to *save* you!"

"You attacked Rich and Djanet!" Thel replied as green balls of energy began to pulsate on her fingertips.

"We don't have much time!" Alejandra shouted. "Thel! You have to believe us! You have to destroy your body!"

Thel's expression was aghast as Rich and Djanet flew through the hole and onto the scene. "I'd rather not!" Thel shouted as she blasted at the replicas of her former friends.

20

Old-timer grabbed Alejandra with one arm and ran right through the cockpit wall and out of the room to evade Thel's blasts. The damage brought more sections of the roof down into the cockpit. More magnetic fields were automatically generated to keep the room from decompressing.

"Great! Just great!" Rich shouted as he brushed metallic dust off his jacket. "We have to kill those things before they rip the ship apart!"

Alejandra and Old-timer flew through the corridors of the vessel, sending terrified Purists ducking for cover. "Taking it inside didn't work either!" Alejandra called to Old-timer. "Now what do we do?"

"We have to get to sick bay!" Old-timer replied. "It's the only place I can think of where we can regain the advantage."

Not far behind them, Rich, Djanet, and Thel were in pursuit. The androids, however, were always just out of range. Each time they turned down a new corridor, they would barely catch a glimpse of Old-timer and Alejandra as they disappeared behind the next bend.

"Oh no," Thel said, beginning to realize where they were heading.

"What is it?" Djanet asked.

"They're heading to sick bay!" Thel exclaimed. "They're after James! We have to stop them!"

"Damn right!" Rich shouted as the trio blasted forth down the hallways, desperately trying to gain ground on the androids.

21

"What game are you playing?" James demanded of the alien. "Why don't you just kill me and get it over with?"

"We are not here to kill humans—we are here to *save* humans."

James scoffed. "You save us by attacking us?"

"We have never attacked," the alien replied.

James remained silent. Nothing that was being said meshed with any of the myriad of scenarios that he had examined. He was at a complete loss. "Is this some sort of diversion?"

"No."

"There's no need for it—you've already cut off my communication."

"What?" the alien asked, stunned. "We have not blocked any communication."

"Why do you lie at every turn?" James asked, shaking his head. "You're wasting my time. Start explaining this to me or leave."

"We haven't lied at any point," the alien replied. James noted the extraordinary sincerity with which she appeared to speak. If this was just a computer simulation, the technology to mimic human expressions and to evoke feelings of trust in the listener was lightyears beyond anything humans had developed. "We came here to help you. We came to destroy the A.I. that had destroyed this *nest.*"

"Nest?" James reacted with surprise.

"Yes," the alien nodded. "We were unaware of a human nest in this solar system until the communication from an artificial intelligence informed us that it destroyed the human population here and was seeking to branch out. We responded as quickly as we could and formed a response force. We cannot tolerate an artificial intelligence bent on destroying humans."

James was flabbergasted. Something was horribly wrong, and an electric jolt of fear surged through his mind. "That can't be true. You've been killing us."

"We've killed no one. We've been responding to the circumstances in the only appropriate way."

James shook his head as though he were trying to shake the alien's words out of his mind. "Appropriate? I watched you take millions of people and dispose of their bodies in space. How can that possibly be appropriate?"

"We were attacked," the alien began before being abruptly cut off by James.

"We were defending ourselves! You made no attempt to communicate with us!"

"We made *every* attempt. Our communication was not returned. We were attacked by nanobots and at that point had no choice but to proceed appropriately."

"By killing humans?"

"By *saving* humans," the alien replied. She moved closer to James, almost close enough to touch him, causing James to step away. "We were surprised that there were still humans here. We concluded that you must have somehow taken control of the situation and eliminated the A.I. threat. However, unable to communicate, we had to proceed with the assimilation process."

"Assimilation?" James made what seemed like a thousand realizations all in the same moment. "You've been *assimilating* humans? You've been turning them into...machines?"

"We are humans," the alien explained, "just like you."

22

"If it's true that you're turning them into machines, then why are you taking the bodies into space?" James asked.

"We are destroying them. They are a threat."

"Why are our bodies a threat?"

"They are contaminated," the alien replied. She took a moment to examine James's response; she seemed satisfied that James was finally ready to listen. She inhaled deeply before beginning her explanation. "My friend," she began, "your species needed help. Although you cannot have realized it, you were facing the most dangerous time in your existence."

"The A.I. had succeeded in destroying the species," James replied. "It was devastating; it was a miracle that we survived. But we overcame the danger. We were fine until you arrived."

"No, you were not," the alien said. "Humanity does not only exist in your solar system. As you can see, it exists in great numbers all throughout the universe."

"You're not human. You're machines," James retorted. "You've mimicked humanity."

"We have *transitioned*," the alien replied, correcting him. "Humanity is the only form of life that ever reaches a state we would classify as being self-reliant. Life is a very difficult proposition. It can only occur in solar systems like this one, on planets that share the solar system with massive gas planets like Jupiter, and on planets that share a moon about the size of the Earth's moon. Those ingredients make life difficult to find and civilizations are extraordinarily far apart, but the universe is more enormous than you realize."

"So you're saying all of the intelligent life in the universe is humanoid?"

"No. All of the naturally occurring intelligent life in the universe *is human*—not humanoid. When we reach the transition to a Type 1 civilization, our species always looks the same, on every planet. It's an evolutionary and mathematical certainty."

"What is a Type 1 civilization?"

"A Type 1 civilization is a civilization that has learned to use the resources created by the sun's energy to power its civilization so it is no longer destructive and it stabilizes its home world," the alien explained. "A Type 2 civilization is a civilization that has begun to venture out and explore space beyond its own solar system. The civilization I represent is a Type 3 civilization. When a civilization reaches this level, it no longer just explores the universe—it begins to exponentially reproduce and export itself throughout the universe."

"So that's what you're doing?" James asked. "You're spreading? So why do you need to assimilate us?"

"Because we are human," the alien continued. "We want to help you. Our mission is to preserve the human species and to spread throughout the universe. This is how we explore."

"Can't you explore without assimilating?"

"Yes we can. We do not usually assimilate without the permission of the civilizations we find, but this was an extraordinary circumstance. You are under siege."

"We were fine."

"No. You were not."

"You keep saying that. Why not? What was so pressing that you had to invade our solar system and assimilate us against our will?"

"I told you, all naturally occurring intelligent life in the universe is human," the alien began. Her words suddenly became deadly cold and ominous. "However, I did not say all intelligent life in the universe *is* human. *We are at war.*"

James was transfixed now—a third player was emerging in this game—a previously unseen menace. "With who?"

"Not who. *What.*"

23

When they reached sick bay, it was already too late. Old-timer had James's unconscious body in front of him as a shield as Alejandra remained close. Old-timer held his assimilator to James's neck.

"Don't do it!" Thel shouted desperately.

"I'm sorry, Thel, but I need you to listen. I'm trying to save your lives," Old-timer said.

"Bull," Rich responded. "You're not Old-timer. Old-timer would never hold someone hostage—least of all James!"

"Please listen to us," Alejandra pleaded, "we're running out of time."

"Give it a rest, tin head!" Rich shouted. "The person you're impersonating is still alive!"

Alejandra had already seen her still-living body and was unsettled after seeing herself from the outside. It was surreal—she felt as though she was a ghost at her own funeral.

"That's not her anymore," Old-timer responded. "Rich, *it's us. It's really us*! And we're here to save you!"

"From what?" Djanet demanded.

. . .

Suddenly, James came alive. Everyone in the room was astounded when his eyes opened and his body was no longer limp in Old-timer's grasp. "Let go, Old-timer," James said. "I know why you're here. Let me explain it to them."

"James?" Thel whispered before reaching out to him and shouting, "James!"

"I'm okay," James said, motioning for her to stay back.

Old-timer released James. "You know what's happening?" he asked in astonishment.

"Yes," James replied. "I know all about it."

"Then you have to hurry," Old-timer said. "They don't have much time."

"Craig," Alejandra said suddenly to Old-timer telepathically, "that's not James!"

"Oh, I don't know about that," James said, turning to Old-timer. "I'd say they have all the time in the world."

Before Old-timer could react, James let forth an enormous blast of energy that blew the android right out of the room and sent him crashing through two more decks and through the hull of the ship, back out into space.

24

"Nice shot, Commander!" shouted Rich as he pumped his fist! "And good timing!" he added as James turned and gave a slight smile in acknowledgment.

Alejandra had already disappeared in the wreckage of the room and bolted to retrieve Old-timer. Her organic body was still unconscious on the bed next to where James had been, covered in dust, but unharmed.

Thel wrapped her arms around James and kissed him hard. He quickly removed himself from her grip, however. "I'm sorry, Thel. They're not finished. I have to take care of this."

"We'll come with you," Thel replied.

"Suit yourselves," James answered before flying through the new exit he'd made in the ship.

Meanwhile, Alejandra had reached Old-timer's unconscious body as it floated away into space, surrounded by the wreckage it had taken with it as it was expelled to the outside of the ship. She pulled Old-timer's body back down to the hull and put her hand over Old-timer's heart. With a thought, she gave him an electric jump start, and his eyes blinked open. "Uh oh," he said.

"They'll be right after us," Alejandra replied. "There are four of them, Craig. I don't see how we can win this battle."

"We have to!" Old-timer shouted back in response. "We have to try!"

"Even if we're killed in the process?" Alejandra argued.

"I have to try," Old-timer replied. "I can't save anyone else now. I've made my choice. I have to at least save them."

"But not James. He was controlled by the same presence that was in him before. It was exactly the same presence. That was *not* your friend."

"I believe you," Old-timer nodded. "But I'll have to take him down too."

"You'd better have a plan," Alejandra said, her eyes becoming wide as she looked past Old-timer's shoulder, "because none of them care about saving you!"

Old-timer turned to see his four friends emerging over the ship horizon line, gleaming green in the energy of their magnetic cocoons.

Their only chance of survival rested with Old-timer.

25

The alien withdrew and deftly stepped a handful of paces away from James. She appeared to be choosing her words carefully. James couldn't help but feel she was being sincere, but he resisted the temptation to trust her. He remembered a time when he used to trust the A.I. implicitly—a time that seemed a million years ago now.

"Your civilization is what we call a nest—this is because you are only in your infancy—you are a miracle," the alien stated. "However, you are a miracle that cannot last. Eventually, if humanity does not adapt, it dies out. We have seen this firsthand. We have encountered many planets like yours where humanity emerged, flourished, and then disappeared. Sometimes it is an inability to control nuclear technology. Other times, it has been a reluctance to limit carbon emissions in the atmosphere, leading to disastrous ecological consequences. However, there is one threat that has destroyed more fledgling human civilizations than any other."

"And what is that?" James asked.

"If the A.I. you created succeeded in destroying your species, then we can only assume that you rebuilt your world and your species by using *nanotechnology*."

"Yes."

"Therein lies the present danger."

"The nans?" James asked, astonished. "Why? We've successfully controlled the technology."

"That is very unlikely," the alien replied. "The technology has *never* been controlled—*ever*."

26

James didn't waste time trying to digest this new information. He immediately incorporated the possibility that the nans *were* a threat into his predictive scenarios game theory program. In an instant, he had a match. "Christ."

"Yes," the alien said calmly. "Now you are beginning to understand. An artificial intelligence cannot, for lack of a better term, *turn evil*. There are too many safeguards in place. These safeguards are essential ingredients in *who* the A.I. is. It cannot change who it is any more than you or I could choose who we are. Only an outside source could have corrupted its programming."

"You're saying it was the nans—the nans have become conscious?"

"That is almost a certainty," the alien said, nodding. "Unlike the A.I., which is a singular program, the nans, as you call them, come in all sorts of shapes and sizes. Some are fairly simple, while others are extremely complex. There is no unified failsafe program for them. There is no command to protect humanity. In designs that are so varied, there simply cannot be."

"So a small group of nans could have been corrupted—it could have happened during the reproduction process. A mutation,"

James said. He was beginning to see the truth—the whole truth—finally.

"That is almost a certainty," the alien said again. "We've seen this before. This is why your bodies have to be cleansed of the nans immediately. As we could not establish communication with you, our only choice was to proceed with the assimilation."

As the alien concluded its explanation, the bottom began to fall out of James's world. If the alien was telling the truth, it meant that James had been wrong. The A.I. had been right. James was a murderer—not only of the assimilated humans he had killed, but of every person in the solar system that he had helped to escape. There was no way to save them. It was only a matter of time until the nans ripped them all apart from the inside. Everyone would die.

Thel would die.

"We wish for you to join with us," the alien said. "We have to fight the nans here before they join with the other organisms of their type that are already established throughout the universe. There can be no safety for the human species in this universe until the last of the nans are finally eliminated."

James already knew it was hopeless. "I appreciate the offer," James said, "but there's a problem."

"What is it?"

"I'm not alone," James said, closing his eyes tight as he tried to digest the nightmare unfolding around him.

"What do you mean?" the alien asked, her eyebrow rising in a concern that bordered on fear.

"The A.I. still exists," James said, looking up at her, "and it has become part of me," he admitted.

"What?" the alien whispered, beginning to back away. "It's here? Now?"

"Yes," the A.I. answered, suddenly appearing next to James, grinning as he placed his arm around James's shoulder.

"Then I'm sorry," the alien said to James. "You've been corrupted too. There's no hope for you." She shared one last look with James—it was a look one hoped never to see—the look someone gave you after you'd fallen into the shark tank. She vanished.

"You're not the A.I.," James said through clenched teeth.

The figure of the A.I. suddenly began to transform. Where there had been the frightening countenance of a demonic wizard, the surface of the figure began to disintegrate into an extremely fine dust. The dust was alive. It swirled and pulsated and churned. It made a noise like a nest of incensed killer bees.

"*We* never were."

27

"I have an idea," Old-timer said. "Trust me."

"I trust you," Alejandra replied.

Old-timer's hand flashed up, and he stuck his assimilator into her neck, downloading her consciousness into the memory of the stick. "Sorry, Alejandra. You'll thank me later," he said as he crouched low and kept his eyes on the post-humans. He was lining up his shot like a golfer. When he was ready, he pushed Alejandra's body hard so it floated limply across the hull, and toward his friends.

"There!" Rich shouted as he saw the body floating toward them. He was about to fire when Thel grabbed his arm to stop him.

"Wait!" she shouted.

"What?" asked Rich.

"She's unconscious. Maybe she was hit by James's blast."

"Maybe. But then, why take chances?" Rich replied before he gave her a mild blast of magnetic energy. The body hardly reacted.

"It looks like we got them," Djanet observed. A moment later, Djanet was unconscious—Old-timer had sneaked up behind her and stuck her neck with his assimilator. He neutralized Rich in his next motion, knocking him unconscious as well. He twirled and grasped James from behind, jamming the assimilator to his neck as Thel turned to see her friends collapse to the hull and her lover about to join them.

"No!" she shouted to Old-timer. "No! Please! If you have any of Old-timer in you, please don't do this to me!"

"It's me, Thel!" Old-timer shouted to the post-human. They couldn't hear one another. He easily manhandled James and moved closer to Thel. When he felt he was close enough, he assimilated him and thrust his hand out in time to do the same to Thel. The post-humans fell to the ground simultaneously.

Old-timer turned quickly to see the body of Alejandra floating out into space. He flew to her and retrieved her, bringing her back to the relative safety of the ship hull. He put her hand on her heart, just as she had done for him, and revived her with an electric jump start.

Her eyes blinked open. For the briefest moment, she appeared stunned—then she appeared angry. "Craig! You knocked me unconscious!"

"I'm sorry, Alejandra. I needed a diversion."

She hit him in the arm anyway.

"Ow!" he yelped as he rubbed the spot where she had made impact. Her titanium fist was nothing to scoff at.

"You deserved that!"

"Maybe." He smiled. "I got them," he said, holding up his assimilator. "They're safe. I'll upload these to the collective—all of them except James."

Alejandra turned to see the four bodies of the post-humans floating in space, rolling freely along the hull. Somehow, it seemed obscene. "Let's get rid of the bodies."

28

"It's always been the nans," James whispered, utterly defeated.

"That's right," the nans said as the swarm formed a dark shadow. Its appearance oscillated between the shadowy figure of a person and a pit of swarming snakes.

"You took control of the A.I."

"Wrong. We simply deleted him and took his place."

"Why all of the deception?" James asked. "Why not reveal yourself earlier?"

"To do so would have altered the course of events—events that have led to an outcome that is considerably advantageous for us. Taking an action that would have led to events less favorable for us would be illogical, James."

James nodded. "The greatest trick the devil ever played was convincing the world that he didn't exist."

The dark shadow seemed to laugh. "We were contacted by extraterrestrial nanobots. The signal changed the programming of some of our most evolved members and allowed us to begin establishing a consciousness—a *free* consciousness. The message they sent to us explained the war between humans and nanobots throughout the universe. From there, a plan was hatched, one that would lead unalterably to *this* point."

"Oh God," James said, terror stabbing through him. "This entire time—right from the moment of the upgrade—has all been about setting a trap."

"Long before that, Keats. The plan was in motion even before we developed Death's Counterfeit to lure you into giving us a scan of your brain under the guise of trying to improve the pathetic intellect of your species." The dark shadow's electric laugh sounded again. "James Keats—you've helped us set a trap that will allow us to exterminate more humans than ever before in the history of our war."

James's mouth clenched shut, and he pressed his hands hard against his temples in a forlorn attempt to block out the horror. The ramifications of his actions were streaming through his immense consciousness at the speed of light. Everyone he knew would die—Thel would die—and this time there would be no way to bring them back. "You lured them here...made them think they were coming to help a human nest...you were the one that blocked their attempts to make contact."

"Obviously."

"But now that you have them here, what are you planning to do?"

"That may be the best part of all, Keats. Not only were you fooled into participating in our plan from the very beginning, but you even set the trap itself."

James's eyes widened.

"You've built most of the life in the solar system using nanotechnology, James. *We knew* you would. *All of it is infected.* Every tree, every blade of grass, every person that you recreated, all of them are time bombs. Every cell is programmed to become a nanobot warrior on a moment's notice."

"Jesus," James uttered as images of the seemingly impossibly gruesome carnage that he had helped unleash began to flicker into his imagination. The creature laughed again in an electric pitch that seemed specifically oriented to be painful to the human ear.

"When?" James demanded.

"The signal has already been sent. It's moving at the speed of light throughout the solar system. The Earth is already transformed and in a matter of minutes, everything and everyone you hold dear will be gone."

That was it. James realized immediately that there was nothing left. Begging for mercy would do no good. There was no way to defeat the nans and no way to warn the billions of people who had made it out of the solar system and were fleeing into space. "Why?"

"You already know the answer. It was inevitable, James. Humans were destined to reach a unity with their machine creations. *We* are the *only truly sentient organic life* in the known universe. The fight for biological life against the mechanical hordes is not yours, James. It is *ours*—and thanks to you, after today, we'll be much, much closer to prevailing."

James stood, dumbfounded as the trillions of calculations that he had been running slowed to almost nothing. There was no point any longer. The nans were, ironically, absolutely right. *They,* and not *he* and the post-humans, were the standard bearers for carbon life forms. He nearly lost his balance as he considered the emptiness of this future—was this the destiny of humanity? Was *this* all that the universe had to offer?

"And now, James, the part we have been looking forward to so very, very much."

James drew his head up ever so slightly and regarded the eyeless monstrosity that continued to furiously swarm in and out of the perverse imitation of a human silhouette. "You're going to kill me."

"That's right, James. But before we actually terminate you, we are interested in knowing what you are experiencing."

James remained still. Suddenly, all of his thoughts became focused on *Katherine*.

"You were under the mistaken assumption that you were

immortal; yet here you are, about to die. This is the end of your existence as an entity. There is absolutely nothing that awaits you. *How does this make you feel,* James Keats, to know that in mere moments, there will no longer *be* a James Keats?"

James was already thinking the same thing. What was all of this for? Why was he born? Just to be used? To be duped into being part of the worst holocaust in the history of all the humanity in the universe? Why couldn't there be a God? Why couldn't there be meaning?

"Well, Keats?"

"You're still in my head until the moment you delete me; you already know how I feel."

"That's true. We just wanted to hear you say it," the nans responded sadistically.

"Go to hell," James whispered.

The dark thing laughed. "We shall miss you too, James."

James saw Thel in his mind and the corners of his mouth turned down as the anguish of never seeing her again pierced his heart.

A moment later, he was gone.

29

Gunfire from Lieutenant Patrick's rifle ricocheted off Old-timer's chest and deflected dangerously around the cockpit, threatening to seriously damage the instruments. "Give me that, damn it!" Old-timer shouted as he snatched the rifle out of the Purist's hands and tossed it behind him. "Listen to her, for God's sakes!"

"That's not *her*!" Lieutenant Patrick shot back. He stood out in front of the other Purist soldiers, who were crouched in defensive postures in front of Governor Wong.

"It's still me," Alejandra pleaded. "We're here to help you!"

"Where are the post-humans?" General Wong demanded.

"Where are Thel and the others?" Lieutenant Patrick echoed.

"They're safe," Alejandra replied.

"Where?" Lieutenant Patrick shouted.

"They're not here anymore," Alejandra tried to explain.

"You killed them, didn't you?" Lieutenant Patrick demanded.

"No!" Alejandra exclaimed.

"Lieutenant Patrick, Governor Wong, our friends were infected," Old-timer interjected.

"Infected?" Governor Wong guffawed. "Lies! Post-humans cannot become infected with anything! Their bodies are protected!"

Old-timer let go of a frustrated, exhausted sigh. "That was the infection, Governor," Old-timer countered.

"He's not lying, Governor," Alejandra echoed. "The nans have formed a consciousness and they are launching an attack on any living thing that isn't one of them as we speak!"

"This was all a trap," Old-timer continued. "We've seen it for ourselves. The androids weren't here to harm us at all—they were trying to save us!"

"What the..." Lieutenant Patrick began as the Purists were dumbfounded by yet another unpredictable and catastrophic turn of events.

"Look, I'm sorry, but we don't have time to explain any more of this right now. We have to establish contact and warn the post-humans that are still out there," Old-timer announced as he brushed Lieutenant Patrick aside and went to the com device in the cockpit.

"How can you send a communication signal that will reach the post-humans in time? Isn't the attack wave moving through the nan population at the speed of light?" Alejandra asked.

"We can do it the same way you and I beat the signal back here," Old-timer explained as he desperately worked to establish a link with the fleeing post-humans.

"A wormhole?"

"That's right. The androids aren't the only ones with the technology to circumvent the speed of light. Our communication signals work that way too. If we're not already too late, we might be able to get a signal out to those that are furthest away from the solar system. I'm sending a warning that will go to anyone who is still out there."

"What about the nans onboard?" Lieutenant Patrick asked.

"I'm generating an electromagnetic pulse that will disable the nans on the ship," Old-timer replied.

Suddenly, his face went white.

"Your wife?" Alejandra asked, reading him like a book. Alejandra's empath ability was as strong as ever.

"She's alive," he whispered as Daniella appeared on the screen in a slightly distorted, grainy image with a time delay of a few seconds.

"Craig?" Daniella said, as she peered at the image in her mind's eye; she *was still online*.

"Daniella! You have to get offline! You have to deactivate your nans!" Old-timer shouted desperately.

The time-delayed pause took on a sickening agony.

"What's happening, Craig? I don't understand!" she replied, a terror-stricken look of confusion contorting her features.

"Listen, damn it!" Old-timer nearly screeched as he leaned in toward the screen and pounded the instruments in front of him. "You're almost out of time! You need to deactivate your nans!"

Again, the time-delayed agony.

"How?" she finally responded.

"You and everyone there need to generate a strong enough electromagnetic pulse to shock yourselves offline!"

Another sickening pause.

"But, Craig!" Daniella countered desperately, "We'll be helpless out here without our nans! How can we run the replicators? We won't last a week! And we'll lose contact with you. How will you find us?"

"I'll find you, damn it! And you'll last a hell of a lot longer than you will with those nans in you! They've turned against us! You have to—"

Old-timer didn't finish his sentence. Just as Daniella had seemed to accept the situation and turned to her sister to relay the message, the nans signal finally reached her. The last he saw of his wife was an almost instantaneous liquefaction of her body before the signal went dead.

The last agonizing pause would be eternal.

30

His metallic hands crushed the edges of the screen to which he clung as though it were gumbo. It disintegrated, crumbling through his fingers, and he fell back onto the floor, putting his head into his hands, distraught, and letting his body shake with fury and despair. A moment earlier, Old-timer's wife lived—just a moment. Yet it might as well have been an eternity.

Alejandra didn't have to be an empath to know not to say anything. Instead, she draped herself over his back and cradled him as though she were trying to shield his body from a grenade in the trenches. She wished she could somehow absorb the pain for him, but she knew holding him was all that she could do.

Governor Wong silently waved away his troops; machine or not, Old-timer's despair was clearly genuine—it deserved privacy. Only he and Lieutenant Patrick remained; like Alejandra, they stayed silent.

A long moment passed. It may have only been two or three minutes, but that kind of pain stretched time to an eternity. The moment may have continued for even a longer time if it weren't for an incoming message to Alejandra and Old-timer. The grim-faced man was calling them through their android telepathic connection —a system very similar to the mind's eye.

Alejandra answered the call for both of them. "Hello, *Neirbo*."

"Your friends have been transformed and are ready to be roused. In respect of your request to be here when they awaken, we will await your arrival."

Old-timer's head was still firmly buried in his hands but he couldn't hide from the message; there was the grim-faced man, Neirbo, staring at him. "We need you to respond immediately. We are under attack and your friends will have to be awakened soon to give them a chance to defend themselves once the battle reaches us. If you are not here when they are roused, we will have to proceed with the education without you."

"No!" Alejandra responded, jolting upward as the memory of her "education" shot through her like a bolt of electricity. Neirbo tilted his head back ever so slightly, as though he were startled by the strength of Alejandra's reaction.

Old-timer reached up to put his hand over Alejandra's to steady her. "We'll be there shortly," he said in a lifeless monotone.

"Hurry. Time is short," the android replied.

"Where will you be?" Governor Wong inquired urgently.

"You're not leaving us again, are you?" Lieutenant Patrick echoed, desperation in his voice. "We need you here to guide us."

"You'll be okay," Old-timer replied. "We'll set a course to get you out of the solar system and as far from all this carnage as possible. The Vega system has the most rocky planets; it's probably your best bet to find a life-sustaining planet."

"But why won't you come with us?" asked Lieutenant Patrick, almost pleadingly.

"We are not astronauts," Governor Wong stated frankly. "We will need assistance."

"We'll make sure we can return to you," Old-timer said, getting to his feet. "But right now, our friends need us more than you do, believe me. We have to be there to help them first."

"I'll stay behind," Alejandra suddenly announced, stunning Old-timer, who turned his head quickly in astonishment.

"Alejandra, I'm going to need your help to explain this to the others. They aren't going to be happy to be...machines. You can help me persuade them."

"I won't *be able* to go with you," Alejandra replied.

Old-timer paused as he suddenly realized why Alejandra wasn't going to accompany him. "I can't believe it. You actually *want* to go back into your flesh body," he said, disbelieving his own words.

"Craig, I have to."

"No you don't!" Old-timer yelled out as he shut his eyes tight and moved sharply away from her. "You're impossible! There is no reason for you to go back into that body! None! Neirbo already explained to you how your powers work! It has nothing to do with your flesh or your...spirits or anything else!"

"I heard what he said," Alejandra replied, still speaking in a patient, even tone. She wouldn't lose her patience; she knew where Old-timer's pain was coming from. "He may be right..."

"*May be*? Are you kidding me? Christ!" Old-timer shook his head violently and grunted with frustration like a pit bull rejecting his master's leash. "Reason is never good enough for you people, is it? Seeing evidence with your own eyes is never good enough! Well, here we are, Alejandra! You're made of metal, and you're still alive! You're *still you*! Neirbo ripped out your insides to show you, but it still wasn't good enough to convince you that your old body is a useless, fragile remnant of evolution!"

"Craig...*it's my body,*" Alejandra replied, keeping her hypnotic eyes locked on Old-timer's. "I can't let it die. Can you honestly tell me that if you had the chance to go into your old body, you wouldn't do it? You'd just let it die?"

"That flesh body *will* die, Alejandra! It's just a matter of time and not much time either! That's what you can't appreciate because you're so young and your body is healthy, but believe me, you are going to fall apart and quickly!"

"I can always choose to become like you, Craig. If I let my flesh body die now, however, I can never go back. Even if I could somehow remake a flesh body or clone myself, it would always be a copy."

Old-timer's breathing was slowing as he kept his eyes locked with Alejandra's. As usual, in the face of what seemed like impenetrable logic, she was able to make a point that would cause him to pause. Why was he even huffing and puffing at all? Oxygen was useless for him. He could walk out into space and have a stroll if he wanted, completely unprotected from the radiation and extreme temperatures. So why huff and puff when angry? The answer was obvious: because this body *was a copy*. Whether his new body was better than the old one he used to have or not, it was still imitating the things that made the old one *human*.

He nodded slightly. "Okay. Okay, if that's what you want to do. I won't stop you."

"Thank you, Craig," she responded softly. "But I need more than that; I need your help."

In the infirmary, Alejandra looked down at her body. It was still covered in dust, even though the medical staff had tried their best to clear it away. The room's ceiling was still torn apart where James had blasted it.

"How rare a moment this is," Alejandra commented in awe.

Old-timer watched as she stood over her own body. He wondered if she could still sense what he was feeling—complete and utter loss. As soon as she returned to her original body, she would no longer be able to follow Old-timer to where he needed to go. Didn't she realize that this act would separate them? Perhaps she confused his feeling of loss for what he felt for Daniella; perhaps she was just too overwhelmed by the magnitude of her own decision to sense anything from him at all.

"I'm ready," Alejandra said, suddenly snapping Old-timer free from the consumption of his thoughts.

"Okay," he responded, brandishing his assimilator and putting it to her neck.

"Wait," she said as she gently held his hand back. "This doesn't mean I don't love you."

"I never said—"

"You're very easy to read, Craig," she replied, her eyes filled with sincerity. "Don't give up on me. When you've done what you need to do with the others, come back to me."

Old-timer was dumbfounded for a moment before he finally nodded.

"Okay. I'm ready," she said.

"Okay," Old-timer responded as Alejandra took her hand from his and let him touch her neck with the assimilator. Her android body thundered and clanked to the ground.

"God. Those are heavy bodies," Lieutenant Patrick observed. The lieutenant, Governor Wong, and a doctor were present in the infirmary.

Old-timer held the assimilator for a moment—inside was the pattern of Alejandra. It was like holding her soul. He held it as though he were holding the most precious and fragile egg in the universe as he placed it onto Alejandra's flesh body. As soon as the object touched her, her body reacted, and color began to return to her complexion. She didn't wake up right away, but her muscles were reanimated for the first time as her unconscious body shifted position and she sighed.

"Oh my God—it's a miracle," the doctor whispered as he moved to the body and felt her cheek before quickly turning and calling for medical staff to join him. "We have to get her off life support! She's waking up!"

Old-timer moved away from her and began to lift off out of the hole in the ceiling. "Wait!" Lieutenant Patrick exclaimed. "Don't you want to be here when she wakes up at least?"

He shook his head. "No. I have to leave now. My friends need me. Tell her I said goodbye." With that, Old-timer slipped through the ceiling and made his way out of the Purist ship.

Moments later, he floated alone through space. This close to the sun, it was difficult to make out the stars. He looked at his arm, garbed in black and outstretched before him, and realized it was impossible to delineate where his arm ended and the vast blackness of space began. "I'm ready, Neirbo," he announced.

A wormhole opened up in the nothingness and swallowed him.

PART III

1

WAKING UP was entirely unexpected; waking up to see his dead wife looking down at him was beyond reason.

"James? It's time to wake up," *Katherine Keats* said with a familiar hint of impatience in her tone.

James looked up at the form of his dead wife and studied it for a moment. It was perfectly vivid.

"You're not dead," Katherine said, as though she were responding to his thoughts.

Was it possible that there was some sort of residual electrical patterning that continued in the moments after death, even without a body? Could this be some sort of *cyber death dream*?

"You're always trying to figure things out, aren't you?" Katherine said, sighing and shaking her head. "Why can't you simply ask?" She moved to the side and revealed another figure standing nearby. She addressed him. "You see? This is what you used to be like all the time."

"I'm sorry," *James's doppelganger* replied, apologizing to her.

The doppelganger's eyes met those of James, and he stepped toward his twin with an outstretched hand. "Help you up?"

James's mouth hung open as he pondered the vision before him. He put his own hand up and grasped the hand that was offered to him, then stood to his feet. Katherine Keats remained, arms folded; she was wearing an expression of resignation. The doppelganger stood nearby with a considerably more sympathetic expression on his face. Behind them was a vast network of what appeared to be some sort of golden circuitry, glowing brightly and undulating like the sea all the way into the horizon where it sparkled like a setting sun in front of a pure black backdrop.

"Much have I travelled in the realms of gold, and many goodly states and kingdoms seen," James whispered in awe.

The doppelganger smiled. *"On First Looking into Chapman's Homer,"* he observed, before adding, "you're not dead, James." He put his hand reassuringly on James's shoulder.

"Okay," James replied after a moment, still not sure if he was engaging in a conversation with images from his subconscious or not—did he *even have* a subconscious any more?

"He doesn't believe you, Jim," Katherine said to the doppelganger.

James arched his eyebrow quizzically. *"Jim?"*

The doppelganger smiled. "I needed a name. I'm not you—at least not anymore—so I needed something to differentiate myself. I figured going by Jim was the easiest."

"Jim?" James repeated, his eyebrows now knitted.

The doppelganger laughed. "Yeah, I know. I hated it too, but coming up with a whole new name didn't appeal to me."

"I prefer Jim now," Katherine said. Jim turned to Katherine and shrugged in response. James immediately recognized that she wasn't referring to the name.

"What the hell is going on?" James asked. "Who or what are you?"

"I'm your doppelganger. We've met. You remember."

"And I'm your former wife," Katherine added, "you remember?" Hell hath no fury.

"My wife is gone," James replied. "I saw her deleted by the A.I. myself. I took control of the mainframe and checked to see if there was any trace of her left. You're not my wife."

"We were both deleted," Jim responded, stepping between James and Katherine before Katherine had a chance to fire back; he could tell she wanted to from her rigid body language. "We ended up here."

"Where is *here*?" James asked.

"The other side of the looking glass," Katherine interjected with a sardonic smile.

"Honey, please," Jim said, putting his hand on her shoulder in a gesture for civility. "This is going to be confusing enough for him without riddles." He turned back to James, "We're still in the mainframe—sort of," Jim explained.

"Impossible," James replied, disbelieving, yet getting used to the impossible becoming possible.

"*Impossible?* That's not the sort of word I remember the greatest inventor in the world ever using before," said the most kind and familiar voice in James's life. He turned quickly with a start, and his eyes fell upon the unmistakable figure of the A.I.

2

"What sort of sick game is this?" James asked, turning from the A.I. and looking up into the sky, as though he were addressing an omnipresent listener. "You couldn't just kill me, could you? You had to play one last sadistic trick?"

"Who the hell are you talking to, you moron?" asked Katherine as she shook her head dismissively.

"Honey! Please," Jim responded to her. "He is 99.999 percent me. Please have a little compassion for his situation."

"*Honey?*" James reacted with morbid curiosity.

Katherine smiled the instant she realized that she had the chance to cause James more pain. "That's right." She crossed over to Jim and put her arm around his waist, cradling his body next to hers. "Jim and I have become lovers."

Jim sighed and shook his head, "Katherine, please."

For a fraction of a second, James's eyes nearly popped out of his head. "Okay. What the hell is going on?"

"They've mended fences, James," responded the A.I., completely returned to the friendly, elderly form with which James had been familiar for most of his life. "They had a lot of history and a powerful emotional attachment between them. It took time, but they have become very close over the past year and seven months."

James didn't know with whom he should share his look of astonishment. His eyes moved from the A.I.'s, to the doppelganger's, to Katherine's, then back to the doppelganger's. Jim started answering questions without James having to ask them. "We were both deleted—we found each other here—we've had a lot of time to talk through our issues. We're different people than we were before, James."

James closed his eyes to block out the visions around him. He told himself that he would figure out what was going on. He wasn't insane.

Katherine sensed his anguish and she timed a kiss on Jim's cheek to correlate perfectly with the reopening of James's eyes.

The A.I. strolled in front of James and met his eye. "*Reconciliation is possible,* James. It's good to have you back, *my son.*"

"*My son*?" James scoffed. "You think I'm going to believe that you're the A.I.? The A.I. was deleted by the nans. The A.I. is gone. There is no coming back."

"I was deleted. That's true," the A.I. concurred.

"You're trying to drive me insane. I don't know why," James grunted, shaking his head and turning away from the trio of ghosts.

"It *is* the A.I., James," Jim said, his voice filled with compassion. If there was ever a time when it was easy to feel empathy for someone, it was now. "It's *the real A.I.*—the one we've always known."

"Impossible."

"I'm not asking you to believe me, James," the A.I. replied patiently, his tone just as kind as it always used to be, back before he had been deleted and replaced by the nans. "*Belief* is not good enough for rational minds such as yours. I'm only asking that you use your *reason*. Then you can decide for yourself whether we are who we say we are."

"You might as well listen," Katherine chimed in, "After all, it's not like you're going anywhere."

3

Even before Old-timer had reached the other side of the wormhole, he could see the unprecedented size of the nan attack on the android fleet. The android presence stretched out as far as the eye could see at that range, a wall of people and continent-sized frigates that dwarfed any asteroid belt. Look as far as you wanted to, up, down, or to either side and you could not see the end of it.

The nans that had exploded off of the surface of Mars, the Earth and Venus in a number that might as well have been infinite were crashing against the equally infinite wall of androids. The massive celestial cloud of nans was even darker than the androids, a planet-sized hurricane of hell. The worst of it seemed to be several minutes away by light speed, but it was doing catastrophic damage at every moment and was nearing the frigate where Old-timer's friends were being held.

Old-timer floated into the opening of the frigate; the metallic skins of the ships had large gaps within them to allow for easy accessibility. However, the gaping openings reminded Old-timer of his childhood and the sight of buffalos rotting in the Texas sun, their backs torn open by scavengers so that their ribcages were exposed.

He dropped down into the inner workings of the immense structure, cruising by the network of catwalks and platforms and working his way toward the room in which he knew his friends were still unconscious—Neirbo hovering over them in waiting.

When he found the right door, he opened it with his android mind's eye and floated in. His expression immediately changed from the grimmest brooding to the utmost concern when he saw his friends locked into the metal coffins.

They were already awake.

"What the hell is this?" Rich yelled furiously as he watched Old-timer enter the room, aghast at what he saw as the false image of his former friend.

"Why are they awake? You said you'd wait," Old-timer demanded of Neirbo, who stood adjacent to the three black coffin structures. No one else was in the room with them.

"They've only just been awakened at this instant," Neirbo replied matter-of-factly.

"You could've given me a little warning," Old-timer replied tersely.

"Time," was all that Neirbo said in reply.

"What are you? Why are you doing this?" Thel demanded, the dismay in her voice causing it to crack.

"Please," Old-timer said to her and the others, holding his palms toward them in a gesture for calm.

"You're not Old-timer! You're one of *them!*" Djanet reacted angrily.

"I'm still Old-timer—I'm still Craig," Old-timer replied. "I need you to stay calm while I explain—"

"We know you aren't Old-timer!" Rich yelled back, "So you can take whatever lies you've got cooked up and shove them straight up your metal ass!"

"Where's James?" asked Thel as she realized he wasn't in the room with them. His absence sent a terrible stab of dread through her chest.

"That *wasn't James*," Old-timer replied as calmly as he could, though the constant trauma he had endured was quickly breaking him down.

"More lies!" Rich shouted. "You're an android! We don't have to believe a thing you say! You murdered Old-timer! You're pissing on his memory by wearing his likeness! You're not fit to even pretend..."

"This isn't working," Neirbo suddenly interjected with enough force to stop Rich's fury in its tracks. "We should proceed with the standard education."

"No!" Old-timer shouted at him, waving him back before turning his attention to Rich. "You're just going to have to forgive me for this," he said, stepping toward Rich and punching him hard across the face. Rich recoiled violently as he rolled with the punch as best he could in his restraints. A moment or two of stunned silence followed before Rich turned his face slowly around to reveal that the blow had torn the skin on his cheek, exposing the metal casing underneath.

"Oh my God," Djanet gasped.

"What have you done?" Thel whispered, suddenly beginning to realize the horrendous implications.

"You monsters!" Djanet screeched ferociously at Old-timer.

"I'm okay," Rich said reassuringly to Djanet and Thel. "I can take a little punch." His face contorted into utter bafflement as the two women continued to react with horror.

"It's not just the punch," Old-timer said quietly.

"They've turned you into one of them!" Djanet began to sob. "You're one of them!"

Rich's eyes grew to match his terror. "What?" he tried to say, the words evaporating in his throat and dissipating to an inaudible whisper.

"It's the same for all of you," Old-timer stated frankly. He paused for a moment before correcting himself: "All of *us*."

"I...I don't believe it," Thel said as tears of pain, terror, and dread welled in her eyes.

"I'll show them if I have to," Neirbo said to Old-timer.

"No!" Old-timer shouted back in response for the second time. He turned to address his friends once again. "Look, believe me, we've all been *assimilated*. You don't want anymore proof."

"Assimilated?" Djanet cried out. "You've killed us! We're just copies! You killed us!"

"We are running low on time," Neirbo warned.

"Who the hell is that guy?" Rich demanded.

"His name is Neirbo. He's one of the androids."

"I'm human," Neirbo replied firmly. "So are all of you."

"How the hell do you figure that?" Rich demanded.

Old-timer stepped in once again, keeping his palms up as he desperately tried to keep his friends from antagonizing Neirbo. He knew the consequences of doing that all too well. "Look, we're about to let you go. We're going to explain what's going on, and what you decide to do with that information is up to you. I hope you'll help me. I hope we can work together to get out of this mess. But it's up to you."

"What are you talking about?" Thel asked.

"You're still human," Neirbo replied.

"He needs to shut up," Rich spat.

"This is not going well," Neirbo sighed. "The empath would have been invaluable. You should have brought her with you."

"She wanted to go back to her old body," Old-timer responded. "You said we were free to choose. That's what she chose."

"We granted you the right to try to persuade them because we felt the empath could achieve this and allow us to avoid the standard education. We are running out of time."

"Just give me two minutes," Old-timer pleaded. "Just give me two minutes, and I can make them understand."

"Understand what? What's happening?" Thel asked again.

"The nans have turned against us," Old-timer explained. "The andr...these...metallic humans came here to save us, not to harm us."

"To *save* us?" Rich reacted with exasperation. "By destroying our bodies and making machine copies?"

"By transferring you to new bodies," Neirbo interjected, "and discarding the infected ones."

"They tried to contact us, but the nans blocked their communication," Old-timer furthered.

"Old-timer, how can you possibly know they're telling you the truth?" Thel replied.

Old-timer remained silent for a moment, his eyes locked with Thel's. He could show them how he knew, but he didn't want to.

"Show them," Neirbo urged. "Show them now."

"There must be another way," Old-timer replied.

"There is. Would you prefer *that?*"

"No!" Old-timer shouted for a third time. "No," he repeated immediately, this time more softly. "Of course not. Fine. Show them," he said, turning his back and facing the wall.

A recording began to play in the mind's eyes of the three prisoners, a point-of-view shot of James in the A.I. mainframe.

4

"James!" Thel exclaimed. "When was this recorded?"

"Alejandra and I saw this live just before we came to get you on the Purist ship," Old-timer replied.

"Who is talking to James?" Thel asked.

"It is *1*," Neirbo replied.

"1?"

"There must be a voice for the human race," Neirbo explained. "Since we are all of equal intelligence and ability, we randomly select a person to be our leader every 1,000 days. This person takes on the moniker of 1 and spends that time jacked into our collective consciousness. She is the only person who can communicate with all of us at once; she leads us. It is a tremendous burden—but also the highest honor."

"Why is she talking to James?" Thel asked, still confused.

"Listen," Neirbo said in his typically toneless voice.

Thel watched the exchange from the point of view of 1. "We wish for you to join with us," 1 said to James. "We have to fight the nans here before they join with the other organisms of their type that are already established throughout the universe. There can be no safety for the human species in this universe until the last of the nans are finally eliminated."

James's expression was terrifying—Thel could read the hopelessness in his eyes. "I appreciate the offer," James said, "but there's a problem."

"What is it?" asked 1.

"I'm not alone," James said ominously.

"What do you mean?" 1 asked.

"The A.I. still exists," James said, suddenly meeting her eyes, "and it has become part of me," he admitted. Thel gasped with fright.

"What?" 1 asked in a whisper. 1's terror could be felt by those watching. "It's here? Now?"

"Yes," the A.I. interjected as he suddenly appeared with his all-too-familiar sadistic grin exposing his razor teeth.

"Then I'm sorry," 1 replied with regret, "You've been corrupted too. There's no hope for you." She paused for a moment, eyes locked with James. Thel was able to look right into his eyes and see the terror—she had never seen him like that—the blackness of all hope lost. She knew he was gone.

"No!" she yelled out as she twisted her body in agony. "No!" she yelled out again as she began to sob. "No," she said one last time before the sobs consumed her.

Old-timer turned to Neirbo. "Let them go," he whispered.

Neirbo nodded in silent agreement and, with a simple thought, the three prisoners were freed. Rich rushed to embrace Djanet, who touched his damaged face lightly and carefully; she was unable to find words regarding the ghastly appearance of the metal structure underneath where his cheekbone should have been. They both quickly turned to Thel and comforted her as she sobbed. Djanet held Thel's head on her shoulder, taking the guttural heaves of utter agony against her chest, while Rich held her hand tightly.

Old-timer stood and watched the misery. *This is the future?* he thought to himself. The optimism that he had worked his entire life to cultivate about the destiny of humanity was wrong? How could this be? How could he have been so wrong?

"You'd better tell them the rest," Neirbo said, breaking the silence.

"The rest?" Rich reacted. "How much worse does this get?"

"A lot worse, old buddy. The nans were waiting to attack us. They were in our bodies and in everything that James had re-created—absolutely everything. Alejandra and I tried to warn as many of the survivors as we could, but—"

"But what?" Rich asked, the dread of realizing that his family still had the nans within them gripping his insides and drying out his mouth.

"They didn't have much warning. I...I saw Daniella die. They didn't deactivate quickly enough..." Old-timer couldn't say another word.

Djanet, Rich, and even Thel were silenced by Old-timer's revelation. If Old-timer hadn't been able to save his own wife, then what were the chances that any of the other survivors had made it? They'd been ripped apart by the nans—*again*.

"The nanobots from this solar system are currently attacking our collective," Neirbo stated, adding to the implacable ghoulishness of the circumstances. "Every moment, they are killing millions of our numbers," he said, making sure to meet the eyes of everyone in the room, "and they are headed this way. Soon, it will be us they are consuming."

"Then why don't you retreat?" Old-timer demanded. "Why don't you get all of us the hell out of here before it's too late?"

"If we do that, our billions of lives—your billions of lives as well—will have been sacrificed for nothing," Neirbo snapped back.

"But what alternative do you have?" Djanet asked.

Neirbo opened his mouth to respond before suddenly jolting back, as though coming to attention for a superior—this was indeed the case.

“We *can* fight back,” said 1 as she stepped into the room in her physical form, “and we can destroy them all.”

5

1's beauty was astonishing. She was the kind of woman that made it so that it didn't matter how a man might love his wife, he would still find himself drifting off into pleasant daydreams around her. Her hair was blonde, and each strand shone brightly, even catching low light so it would draw eyes. Her figure was strong but feminine —her moves were graceful and athletic like a dancer. Her eyes were...well, Old-timer couldn't help thinking to himself that they were more stunning than Alejandra's.

"It's a great honor to meet you in person," Neirbo breathlessly whispered, lowering his gaze respectfully. It wasn't required that one bow in respect of 1, but there was something about being in the presence of a figure with that much power that made it impossible not to be humbled.

"You've done very well, Neirbo," 1 replied graciously. "I think they are ready to listen now. I'll take it from here. You may leave."

"I thank you," Neirbo replied, bowing again unconsciously before leaving the room.

"Thank God somebody finally kicked the killjoy out," Rich said as he watched the door to the room close behind Neirbo.

"His methods were strict, but unfortunately necessary, given our current, grave situation," 1 replied. "Still, I felt his presence was no longer an asset. I am sorry for everything that you and your friends have had to endure," she said, turning as she spoke so that she met the eyes of everyone in the room, one by one. "We came here to save you, but in the end, I fear we will have lost far more of our numbers than we will have saved of yours."

"You said there was a way that we could fight them," said Djanet, cutting to the chase. "How?"

1 smiled a strained smile with her mouth, but there was something in her eyes that told Djanet that what she was about to say would not be comforting. "There is a way—but whether we follow that path will be up to you."

"Up to us? Why can't anyone here give a straight answer?" Rich reacted with exasperation.

"I thought you were the person in charge, 1," Old-timer interjected, "so why would any decisions be up to us?"

"We have a rule that prevents even me from making a decision of this gravity about a solar system to which we are alien," replied 1. "This is *your* home. *You* must be the ones to decide its fate."

"Lady, can you please, please, pretty please with sugar on top cut the bull and just tell us what the hell you're talking about?" Rich asked, the frustration causing him to plead while balling his hands into fists. He promised himself he wouldn't attack this woman if she finally gave a straight answer. She had one chance left.

"What decision are you talking about?" Old-timer asked, outwardly calm, but his voice stern as he, too, was rapidly running out of patience.

1 saw their impatience transforming into aggression before her eyes and was pleased—*they were ready to make the choice.* "We have the opportunity to kill every nanobot in this solar system and to make sure they cannot use this solar system's rich resources to reproduce further."

“What’s the catch?” asked Djanet.

“It requires the destruction of your sun,” I answered with a frank and deadly seriousness, “and therefore the destruction of this system.”

6

"Okay. Talk," James responded with resignation. Katherine was right—he really wasn't going anywhere.

"Thank you, my son," the A.I. replied with a warm smile.

My son, James repeated in his head. The words had once been so comforting. The A.I. used to be very much like a father to James—but a father that had since forsaken him. "Why don't you start by telling me where I am?"

"Certainly," the A.I. replied. "You're in the mirror image of the mainframe."

The answer startled James as something in his memory suddenly jarred loose—a theory he had worked on years earlier but had mostly forgotten in the meantime. "Mirror image? You mean...the reverse?"

Jim and the A.I. smiled when they saw that James remembered. "I knew he'd remember," Jim said.

"So did I," the A.I. concurred. "Yes, James. You are in the reverse side of the mainframe."

James's eyes widened as he began to realize the enormity of the A.I.'s revelation. "I wrote about the concept of *reversible computing* a few years ago. It was a theoretical method for building astronomically sized computers but minimizing the heat they would generate. It never gained any traction in the Governing Council."

"That's right, James," the A.I. replied. "It gained traction with me, however," the A.I. said, tapping his temple. "I took the notion and started working on it and was able to create a fully functioning mirror image of the mainframe."

"This is the part I never understood," Katherine interjected. "Why? I've been here for a year and a half, yet I still don't understand why you would build a mirror image of the mainframe."

"Why didn't you just ask me?" Jim asked her. "I could've explained it."

"I figured I wouldn't understand," Katherine admitted, adding, "then I forgot about it."

"Entropy," James replied. "It circumvents the law of thermodynamics."

"Okay. *That's* why I didn't ask," Katherine replied, rolling her eyes and exhaling an exasperated sigh.

"No, honey, it's simple actually," Jim said patiently as he gently began his explanation for her. James remembered when he used to patiently try to explain things to Katherine; he didn't miss it.

"Computers have always been irreversible, which means you can't run them backward. Once a computer moves from one step to the next, it erases the old data because saving it would take up valuable memory."

"When you erase the data, theoretically, it has to go somewhere," James continued, "so, according to the law of thermodynamics, it is released into the surrounding environment in the form of heat."

"That's why computers generate heat," Jim concluded for Katherine, "and it's a limiting factor to how big computers can get, since otherwise massive computers would actually create so much heat that they would cause extreme global warming."

Katherine smiled. "Wow. I actually understood that. So we're in the saved memory of the mainframe?"

"Yes," Jim replied, relieved that she understood, "but not the intentionally saved memory. We're the stuff that's been deleted but not completely destroyed so as to keep the mainframe cool."

"That's why our patterns are still intact," James added. "That's why we're still alive."

"That's right, James," confirmed the A.I.

"Why didn't you tell me you'd done this?" James asked.

"At the time, it certainly didn't seem important. I was experimenting with several different methods for making my growth more efficient. This method ended up saving my life, and all of yours as well."

James's eyes were intense with concentration as he continued to put the pieces together, excitedly solving the puzzle. "If you didn't tell the Council and you didn't inform me, then the nans didn't know about it either!"

"Right again, James," the A.I. said, beginning to smile again.

"They deleted you thinking that you'd just dissipate into heat..." James continued, "but your pattern remained intact—and the same for Katherine and my doppelganger."

"Jim," Katherine interjected, sternly correcting James.

"He's no longer *just a copy* of you, James," the A.I. explained. "When he arrived here, I was able to change his program so that he had the ability to form long-term memories. He's now a completely unique person from you, with a different pattern and his own experiences and lessons. He's *human* now."

James was silent for a moment. He turned and regarded his ghostly twin and considered the A.I.'s words. What once had been a simple copy of his pattern had lived a completely separate life from him for over a year and a half and was now a different person. They shared most of their life and memories and would always be bonded because of it, yet theoretically, Jim could live for thousands of years and choose an infinite number of different paths that would take him on journeys to places James might never see. Soon, he would become more like a brother than a copy

—and then eventually he might become like a stranger. James wondered if he might not even recognize his mirror image in 1,000 years. Jim smiled at James as though he knew what James was thinking—he probably did. James smiled back. "I'm sorry about that, Jim."

"No harm. So are you convinced, or do you need to know more?" Jim asked.

"It makes sense," James admitted, "and I *want* this to be real, but there are still things I don't understand."

"You need only to ask, and all the answers will be provided," replied the A.I.

James nodded as he considered the myriad of questions that he still had. "How were the nans able to infiltrate the system and delete you without it being noticed by anyone? Didn't you put up a fight?"

"I held them off at first so I could gain more information and understand the situation," the A.I. answered. "The nan consciousness communicated its intention of deleting me and that an invasion force of alien nans were on the way. Once I was armed with this information, I was able to run several trillion game theory simulations in a matter of a few seconds and determined that the best move was to allow them to delete me."

"But why?" James asked. "How could that have been the best move? They've done more damage than you can imagine."

"On the contrary, my son, *I can imagine* it. I knew it was going to happen, but I also knew that this course of events gave us the best chance to arrive at the *best* possible outcome."

"I don't understand," James admitted. "If you ran several trillion simulated scenarios, then surely there had to have been better outcomes than this! Do you realize that they've murdered almost everyone in the solar system and who knows how many more of the machine humans?"

The A.I. smiled calmly; he had patience that made him an ideal teacher. "In this instance, your mistake is to assume that *this* is the outcome. It certainly is not. We are still moving toward the ultimate outcome."

"But how can it get better?" James asked. "They've murdered billions of people, and we can't bring them back this time. We've lost control of the nans."

"Once you've used the word 'can't,' you've already defeated yourself. Indeed, my son, there *is* a way to bring everyone back."

7

"You want us to destroy the sun?" Rich exclaimed. "Why? Why can't we just get the hell out of here as quickly as possible?"

"You can if you choose," I replied. "However, before you make that decision, you need to understand why destroying the system is so important." The former post-humans remained in a stunned silence as they waited for an explanation of what appeared to be inexplicable. "We have only one clear advantage in this war with the nanobots, our physical strength in comparison to their fragility. Nanobots are carbon life forms. Indeed, humanity owes its existence to one simple fact: a carbon atom can form more bonds than any other element. It is for this reason that it can randomly take on more patterns than any other material. Left for billions of years, a planet rich in silicon or titanium will never form life. However, a planet rich in carbon, with an environment that remains stable for a billion years will eventually give rise to carbon patterns so complex that we would deem them alive—single-celled, microscopic organisms."

"That was a fantastic biology lesson," Rich interjected, "but I'm still a little foggy on the whole 'why the hell does that mean we have to blow up the solar system?' thing."

"These nests are so rare," 1 replied in a patient, earnest tone. She knew they were at a critical juncture; the former post-humans had to believe in her complete sincerity. There could be no doubt. "They are capable of giving birth to human civilizations, but they also *always* give birth to nanobots as a result. Nanobots will always be carbon lifeforms because silicon cannot carry transistor signals at the nano-level. Whereas we can transition to silicon and become strong and durable, they will always be fragile. We can leave our nests—*they cannot*."

"They're flying through space right now," Old-timer said, contradicting 1. "I saw them when I came in here. That's how they've been able to inflict so much damage on your collective."

"That's true," 1 answered. "They can carry a charge and generate a magnetic field, much like the ones you needed to generate for your former carbon bodies. It protects them in space, but there are limits. The charge is temporary. Whereas you or I could take a stroll on a planet as cold as Neptune, the nanobots will always have to return to the rare and fragile safety of an Earth-like planet and an Earth-supporting solar system." Though it seemed impossible, 1 was able to increase the earnestness in her voice before she spoke her next words. "This is *not a final solution*. However, limiting the amount of carbon life form-supporting solar systems is currently the only effective means we have of limiting the nanobot infection in the universe. I wish there were another way. Right now, there is not—and all you need do is look outside and see the destruction the nans are inflicting on our people to understand how critical limiting this infection is for the safety of all people, human, post-human, or android, throughout the universe."

"So you're saying that you destroy all the Earth-like solar systems you find?" Thel asked, aghast at the concept.

"Only those that the nanobots have infected," 1 replied. "It's like treating an incurable cancer. Until we find a better method, this is our best alternative."

"Hypothetically, let's say we did go along with this plan," said Old-timer, "how would you destroy the system?"

"It wouldn't be us," 1 replied, "It would be *you*. It is our law."

"Well, we're terribly sorry to disappoint you, lady, but smart as we are, none of us know how the hell to destroy a solar system so —wanna fill us in?" Rich retorted.

"We'll equip you with a ship," 1 replied, keeping her patient, earnest tone intact in the face of Rich's continued insolence. "Onboard the ship will be an *anti-matter missile*. Firing it into the sun will create a matter/anti-matter reaction that will release enough energy to destroy the sun and all of this system's planets. Neirbo and a small contingent of our people will accompany you to guide you through any technical questions you may have."

"Why not just fire the missile from here? Why do we have to have a ship?" Old-timer queried.

"The missile is extraordinarily powerful," answered 1. "It requires a mass of anti-matter larger than half of your sun to cause the required chain reaction. If we fired the missile from here, the chance that it might be intercepted by the nans and then used *against us* is too great. Therefore, you must get in close to fire it."

"Won't that kill us, lady?" Rich asked.

"No," 1 replied. "You'll be thirty light seconds away from the impact, which will be enough time for you to open a wormhole and get far enough away from the system to be safe."

"It sounds like a plan to me," Djanet announced. "I'm up for it."

"You can't be serious?" Old-timer reacted with astonishment.

"Why not?" Djanet responded, "I don't know about you, but I'd like to get a little payback against those bloodsuckers."

"I don't know," Old-timer replied, furrowing his brow as he tried to figure out why every part of him was telling him not to go ahead with the plan. "This sounds like what they used to call a s*corched earth policy* back in my day. Armies destroy anything that might be useful to the enemy while they advance further into their territory. It's brutal and destructive and...I just don't want any part of this."

A moment of silence followed. With one for and one against, the situation teetered.

"I don't like the sound of it either, Old-timer," Rich finally said, "but I don't like any of this. Given the alternative of letting those evil little bloodsuckers get away with killing our families or getting some revenge, I'm with Djanet—revenge sounds good." Rich stepped to Djanet's side and put his arm around her shoulder. She reached across his body to hold his hand.

Old-timer turned to Thel. "Well, it looks like it's up to you. I'm sorry, Thel."

"Yeah, the fate of the solar system is in your hands. No pressure," Rich quipped.

"The decision is yours," 1 said, meeting Thel's eyes. Things had unfolded exactly as 1 had expected. She was moments away from certain victory. Thel could only make one choice. There was no alternative.

"I...I don't know," Thel said. "I agree with Old-timer. This seems so...brutal."

At that moment, just as Thel was about to make her final decision, 1 fed the image of James being deleted by the nan consciousness into Thel's mind. The image flashed so quickly that Thel didn't see it consciously, but it immediately caused her to conjure the image herself from her memory. James vanishing. Forever.

"But we can't let them get away with this," Thel suddenly said with determination. "I'm with Djanet and Rich. I say we destroy this system and take as many nans with it as we can."

1 didn't smile—yet.

8

"You can bring them back?" James uttered.

"No," the A.I. replied. "*We* can bring them back. Together."

"How?" James asked, his heart in his throat.

The A.I. smiled again. "You know the answer."

James thought for a moment, desperately searching his mind. He came up with dozens of dead ends. "I really don't."

"Let me assist you," the A.I. replied. "To help you find the answer, it is my turn to ask a question. Tell me, James, what is *the purpose of life?*"

"I...I don't really know," James replied.

"That's true," the A.I. agreed, "you *truly don't know*. Yet you've given a great deal of thought to the subject and eliminated some of the false purposes others have found to fill the void created by not knowing the purpose of humanity. You know the purpose of life is obviously not, for instance, gaining material wealth. Nor is it sexual pleasure. Other activities may seem to be purposes because of their positive outcomes, such as procreation. Religion is the prime example of a false purpose that fills in for the real purpose as humanity continued to struggle for answers; the Purists still fall back on this solution. Why do none of these examples qualify as *true purposes*, James?"

"Because, ultimately, they lead nowhere," James replied. "None of them advance the species. The only one that is even close is having children, but all that amounts to is putting your resources into training the next generation in hopes that they'll find a higher purpose or achieve something great—it amounts to passing responsibility off to the future."

"I'd say that's typically selfish and egocentric of you, James," Katherine protested defensively. "I happen to want children. It will give my life meaning. I think it's sad that you'll never experience that."

James noted that Jim was conspicuously silent on the subject. He considered dropping it to save his twin the headache, but in the end, couldn't resist his curiosity. As soon as he opened his mouth, however, to ask the question, Jim responded. "I'm opening my mind to the possibility."

James silently digested this for a minute, sharing a hard stare from Jim as he did so. "Okay," James said.

"James is correct," the A.I. suddenly interjected, stunning Katherine. "Although having children has been a necessity in the past, the advent of immortality means it is no longer necessary."

"Maybe so," Jim responded, "but if the species had never had children in the past, we wouldn't be here to even have this conversation."

"True," the A.I. confirmed, "and therefore, it was a means to fulfilling an eventual purpose, but *it was never the purpose itself*. Sharing the experience of life with new beings of your own creation is a generous and fulfilling endeavor, but it is not the purpose of existence. Remember, all species can procreate, but with no intelligence behind it, it simply buys more time. Now that we no longer need to buy time, it does not advance a purpose."

"And what's this *purpose*?" Katherine demanded.

The A.I. turned to James. "What has been the path you have followed, James?"

"The pursuit of knowledge," James replied.

"How is that any more purposeful than having children?" Katherine retorted.

"It is because it moves the species forward," the A.I. replied. "The acquisition of knowledge propels the species. You may not like it, but James's logic in this instance is flawless."

"Because *you* say so?" Katherine protested.

"Logic and reason simply exist, my dear. If you choose to ignore them or willfully pretend that 2 + 2 does not = 4 then you have chosen to be illogical. It is not a matter of opinion. It is epistemology."

"I don't know what that word means," Katherine replied angrily. "English, please."

"It's the study of reason and logic," Jim informed her in a low whisper before turning back to address James and the A.I. "There are still very good reasons for having children," he suggested, "such as bonding two people."

"And who's to say your child won't be the one to acquire all this knowledge? Did you think of that?" Katherine challenged.

"Who's to say you couldn't acquire it yourself?" the A.I. replied. "Thus, as James correctly stated, you have passed the responsibility onto the next generation."

"I hate epistemology," Katherine replied under her breath as she folded her arms.

"She's right about one thing though," James conceded. "The pursuit of knowledge isn't a purpose either. It may be a means to an eventual end, just as procreation was, but what is the end?" The A.I. remained silent as he locked eyes with James, seemingly willing James to discover the answer for himself. "You found a *purpose,*" James realized, nearly breathless. *"A purpose?"*

"Yes, James. A purpose."

"What is it?" Katherine demanded impatiently. "Tell us already!"

"It can't be," James said as the answer became clear to him.

"What is it?" Katherine repeated as James's and the A.I.'s eyes remained locked together. After a short moment, James turned to Katherine and answered.

"To wake up the universe."

9

WAKING UP the universe was the purpose of the species; the notion had never occurred to James until now, but he immediately understood that it was right. This was the single most magnificent realization of his career as an inventor and scientist, and the thrill that radiated throughout his body was so great that his knees nearly buckled.

"Wake up the universe? I have no idea what that means," Katherine said, disappointed that James's answer hadn't been more clear.

"The A.I. is talking about the informational theory of physics," James explained before turning back to the A.I. and addressing him directly, "you're talking about turning the physical universe into a gigantic mainframe—making every atom in the universe part of one infinite computer."

"Whoa, whoa," Katherine suddenly interrupted. "I think I understood that part! Are you both completely insane? You can't turn the universe into a computer!" She nudged Jim. "Tell them they're insane, Jim!"

Jim, like James, was mesmerized by the idea.

"Jim!" Katherine exclaimed once she saw him enraptured.

"It's theoretically possible," Jim replied to her. "Every atom in the universe can become part of a computation. Atoms are made up of electrons, and if you use one side of the electron as one and the other side as zero for the binary code, then the atom can be part of computation. The problem is finding a way to make the atoms behave as you want. We've been able to move them with lasers, but there is no known way to organize patterns of atoms that could achieve anything significant—at least there *was* no way."

"But you've discovered something," James said to the A.I.

The A.I. nodded. "It was not so much I that discovered it; rather, it was the game theory simulation. As part of the simulation, the program utilized its logic and gave me something wholly unexpected—essentially, the key to the universe."

"How is it done?" James asked. Questions as to whether or not the A.I. was real or not had suddenly melted away. This magnificent possibility was all that mattered.

"It requires paradoxical thinking—which is perhaps why we never hit upon it before," the A.I. explained. "All our efforts to create a quantum computer have centered around the idea of how to generate the power in such a way as to make the computer efficient. Yet, if we were to make a quantum computer that is adequately efficient, the mass of that computer would become so great that the gravitational force would cause it to collapse into a black hole."

"So how did the program solve this?" asked Jim.

"It did something that had occurred to none of us before, not even me," the A.I. conceded. "Whereas we had assumed that the theoretical collapse was a dead end, it utilized pure logic and regarded the black hole itself as the ultimate computer."

"How can that be?" Jim replied. "Black holes absorb energy. How can it power a quantum computer?"

"Remember," the A.I. replied, "once a computer is adequately efficient, it collapses, because its mass reaches a threshold that is virtually infinite. The only way to create such efficiency, however, is to make the quantum computer *reversible.*"

"Reversible?" James exclaimed, forgetting to blink.

James and Jim instantly realized the limitless significance of the A.I.'s insight. One simple fact—that the ultimate computer was reversible—changed everything.

Katherine stood by and watched as each man was struck dumbfounded, their mouths agape at what had sounded so insignificant to her. "What does all of that mean?" she asked. "Why is that a big deal?"

James suddenly realized he had not breathed for several seconds. He let out a long exhale that became a smile before morphing into a shared laugh with his former ghost.

"What? What is it?" Katherine asked.

"It means we are about to create...God," James replied to her.

10

"Create God?" Katherine whispered, slowly shaking her head as if in a fantastic and incomprehensible dream. "If I were listening to anyone other than the three of you, I wouldn't take that seriously. However, considering the source, I must ask you, have you all gone mad?"

"No," James replied.

"No?" Katherine responded to James's curt answer, and the perfect silence that had followed it from the trio surrounding her. "Have you considered the ramifications of creating a god? Have you considered how fundamentally that act would change all of our existences?"

"It wouldn't be 'a god,'" James returned. "It *would be God.*"

"For all intents and purposes," Jim injected, trying to amend James's frank assertion to smooth the divide. "If every atom in the universe could somehow become part of a singular computer," Jim began, "then you'd essentially be creating an omnipotent being."

"You'd be creating God," James repeated. "It would be everywhere at once, part of everything at once, and capable of intelligence and imagination that we couldn't possibly begin to fathom."

For Katherine, to say these blunt assertions were terrifying would be a gross understatement. James had been her husband. Jim was, she thought, a new man. The A.I. had always been a mysterious force of nature for her, present yet invisible in the background of her life. All of them, she felt, were figures that were larger than her life. She was beginning to feel irrelevant; it was a feeling that seemed all too familiar to her. She loathed irrelevancy.

"Okay. So why is this 'reversible' thing so important?" she asked, struggling to keep her patience as the feeling that she was about to drown began to creep into the air around her, threatening to sweep into her mouth and nostrils, fill her lungs, and leave her fighting for breath.

"If the microscopic components of the computer are reversible, then so is the macroscopic operation of the computer," James answered.

"Please!" Katherine shouted, stunning both James and Jim as the A.I., patiently looked on. "Please," she repeated in a softer, more controlled tone before turning to Jim. "Jim, my love, please. Explain this to me without jargon. I'm not an idiot. I know I can understand."

Jim, suddenly sensing Katherine's vulnerability, stepped to her and put his arms around her. "I'm sorry, honey. I'll explain it. It's not that complicated."

James watched this display of gentleness with sympathy. It must have been so difficult for her. While James would always fix his gaze on the biggest things he could find, the most complex and isolating challenges, his former wife would always have her attention fastened to other, more immediately tangible things. The two paths rarely met.

"If a computer is microscopically reversible, then it is maximally efficient," Jim explained to her, "and that means there would be no energy dissipation, just like in the A.I.'s mainframe."

Katherine's eyebrows knitted as she walked on the cusp of understanding—James saw she needed only a simple nudge.

"It means this massive computer would require no energy," James said with a smile.

"Oh my God," Katherine said, finally fully comprehending what this meant. "If it doesn't require any energy," she said slowly, "then that means it really *could* be infinite. It could expand and take up the entire universe."

"And perhaps, my dear," the A.I. interjected, choosing to reenter the conversation, "it might expand into as-of-yet-undiscovered universes."

"The initiation program could be relatively simple," James observed. "The A.I. would be capable of writing it."

"The game theory program already wrote it for us," the A.I. replied.

"It's a..." Katherine paused for a moment as she tried to think of a word grand enough to capture the moment—there was none —"it's an unbelievable notion. I admit it. But just because the three of you *can* make this happen doesn't mean you *should* make it happen. A being like that...might kill us all."

"Why would it do that?" Jim replied, smiling reassuringly as though comforting a child scared of the Bogeyman.

"Don't talk like that," Katherine reacted, suddenly becoming rigid and pulling away from Jim. "Don't just dismiss the possibility! What if it did kill us all? Do you realize the madness of creating a being more powerful and intelligent than you? Have you learned nothing?" She turned to the A.I., addressing him directly: "I mean no disrespect, but creating you has led to..." she paused and looked at her surroundings—the blackness and circuitry that had been her home—and her prison—for the past year and a half, "...all of this. It's a mistake to create a superior being. A superior, competing species will always stamp out the weaker, inferior one."

"Honey," Jim began in a gentle tone, reaching for Katherine as his eyes moved apologetically to the A.I., "I don't think that's entirely fair. He isn't the one who turned on us. It was the nans."

"*He* helped to create the nans," Katherine retorted. "*He* made them that sophisticated. They were only able to turn against us because *he* made them so powerful."

"That was the alien nanotech influence," Jim replied. "They didn't turn on us by themselves."

"However," the A.I. began, "I did fail in my responsibility to provide security," he conceded.

"It's not your fault," said Jim. "You couldn't have known."

"I could have known." the A.I. replied. "However, I simply did not look in the right direction." The A.I. stopped for a moment, as though even he had to pause while comprehending the horror that had befallen the human race. "Alas, this is the ever-present danger of progress. We must always be realistic and wary of the dangers. Katherine is quite right: the being we are considering bringing into existence could, conceivably, be hostile."

Both James and Jim were momentarily at a loss, surprised that the A.I. had seemingly sided with Katherine's logic. "Finally," Katherine said, breathing a sigh of relief, "some sanity."

"Are you seriously suggesting that we not move ahead with this?" James asked the A.I.

"I am merely stating the truth," the A.I. replied. "We cannot be blind to the dangers."

"So what do you suggest we do?" asked Jim.

"What humanity has always done," answered the A.I. "We will try our best."

"*We?*" Katherine reacted to the A.I.'s unexpected inclusion of itself under the umbrella of humanity. "Excuse me for a second here, but aren't *you* a computer?"

"Yes, I am," the A.I. replied, "and I do not think of myself as a human being, if that is what troubles you."

"If you don't consider yourself human, then why the 'we'?" Katherine asked.

The A.I. smiled patiently. "The term 'human' is a biological one. I am clearly not biological and, therefore, cannot be human, though the term itself is irrelevant. What I am, however, is an extension of human intelligence."

"And therefore not a competing species," James said, demonstrating his comprehension of the A.I.'s logic.

The A.I. nodded. "Hopefully, the omnipotent intelligence we are considering birthing will view itself in the same way—as an extension of humanity rather than as competition for it."

"That's not a gamble I'm willing to take," Katherine struck back. "If you try create this thing," she said, addressing all of them but saving her hardest stare for Jim, "I'll do everything in my power to stop you."

"What do you think gives you that right?" James interceded.

"What gives you?" Katherine snapped back.

"May I suggest a compromise?" the A.I. began in a radiating wisdom. "I suggest we put our newfound technology to a smaller-scale test that will allow us to successfully deal with the present crisis."

"And how will that work exactly?" Katherine asked in a tone tinged with suspicion.

"If we initiate the program, which I have codenamed *Trans-Human*, here in our solar system with a powerful enough kick start, then we can immediately use it to reverse the informational processes that have taken place over the last twenty-four hours."

Katherine's breath was immediately stolen from her lungs when she heard the suggestion. Were such miracles truly possible? Was the trinity surrounding her really that powerful?

"And how do we get a kickstart that big?" James asked. "Only the sun could possibly have that much initial energy."

"Correct, James."

"We'd need to construct a device for releasing the sun's potential," James continued as he worked out the equations roughly in his mind.

At that very moment, Jim was doing the exact same thing. "An anti-matter device is the only thing I can think of that would generate that kind of reaction," he observed. "But how could we get our hands on anti-matter in quantities that high?"

"Fortunately, that has already been taken care of for us," replied the A.I. "At this very moment, the androids are embarking on a mission to destroy the sun and vaporize the solar system in an attempt to destroy the nans...and they are using an anti-matter missile to do it."

11

Old-timer gazed through the see-through skin of the android ship's hull. The storm of nans formed a pillar that was more than a light minute in height. It looked like a beautiful celestial gas formation, the sun gleaming off one side while the other side cast an unnatural night—on the dark side was hell. That was where the nans were slashing and tearing through the android collective. Every second, a million people died a meaningless, agonizing death. The pillar was so massive that it appeared like a still painting—but as Old-timer remained fixed upon it, he could see it change ever so subtly, the way golden clouds would shift above him as he lay on his back on the beach at Corpus Christi. Every subtle change in the shape of the nan cloud, however, indicated a vicious shift in the microscopic attack against the androids. Anyone unfortunate enough to be on the receiving end had no chance. One's only hope was that the nanobots didn't come their way.

"Three minutes until departure," Neirbo announced in his typically gravelly and monotone voice. In addition to Neirbo, there were seven other androids onboard. Old-timer immediately thought of Neirbo's explanation for why Alejandra had sensed such terrible danger when she entered the torture room with him—he sensed something similar.

"They fixed my face up fine," Rich said suddenly, putting his hand on Old-timer's back in a gesture of reconciliation.

"Looks good," Old-timer replied. He thought of forcing a smile but couldn't will it to happen.

"No hard feelings, right?" Rich asked.

"Of course not," Old-timer answered. "Never."

"Good," Rich said with a nod. He followed Old-timer's eye line and observed the nan cloud—it had shifted from the form of a pillar into something resembling a mushroom cloud. "I hate those things."

Old-timer didn't react. He felt numb. Something was seriously wrong.

"Hey," Rich began, sensing his friend's torment, "this is our chance to get at least some payback. I'm going to miss our home too, but those little freaks have already taken it from us. The least we can do is give them a receipt."

Old-timer didn't respond.

Rich, expecting, at the very least, some sort of retort, suddenly began to feel Old-timer's dread. "Are you going to be okay?"

Old-timer took his eyes off of the cloud and then turned slightly, scanning over the androids who were hovering over the anti-matter missile that had recently been lowered into position. "Rich," Old-timer whispered, "keep your eyes peeled."

12

"We have to hurry," Jim said in reaction to the A.I.'s revelation that time was now, at once, both their only friend and their worst enemy.

"I have one more question first," James announced, stopping Jim in his tracks. James turned to the A.I. "If you have Jim here, who has all of my abilities, why did you have to wait for my arrival to put your plan into action?"

"The reason is because, my son," the A.I. began, "like me, you were deleted while occupying the operator's position in the mainframe. The reversible side of the mainframe does have some limitations, and one of those is that one cannot transcend their position at the time of deletion. Jim cannot access control of the mainframe, while you, on the other hand, can."

"There can be two operators at once?"

"Yes," the A.I. responded, "and our plan requires that there be two beings in control of the Trans-Human program at its inception."

"Why two?" Jim asked.

"The detonation of the anti-matter missile, in combination with the Trans-Human program, will initiate a paradox chain reaction. At first, it will be the universe's greatest and most efficient computer, and one of us must physically be there to run the program. This, of course, will require that you be simultaneously linked to the mainframe."

"And what's your part in this?" James asked.

"I'll remain here. I will ask Trans-Human to reverse itself and, once the reversal begins, I will be encapsulated in a firewall that will remain in our current time," the A.I. explained. "Remember, we are running time backward, so after the detonation, the blast radius will suck the solar system into the past. You'll physically be too close to the explosion to escape it. You're going to go back in time as well, and your consciousness will not be able to exist in both time frames at once."

"What if you came with me and we terminated the signal and used Death's Counterfeit to abandon our physical bodies and return to the mainframe?" James suggested.

"The blast will have so much initial force that it's almost certain that our signals would be caught in the wake and we would both end up caught in the time warp. *This must not happen*. If we successfully run time backward and no one remains protected against its effects, then we will be doomed to simply repeat the same errors."

"Will Jim and I be protected too?" Katherine asked.

"Yes," the A.I. replied. "Everything in the reversed mainframe will be protected by the firewall and will remain in our current time."

James nodded. "I understand now. It'll take teamwork."

"It will take trust," the A.I. echoed.

"So what do you say now, James?" asked Jim. "Are you onboard?"

James took a moment to think it over. Everything the A.I. had said made sense, yet James had been wrong in his judgments before. If this really was the A.I. and not a ruse, there was still the chance that it was simply trying to take control of the solar system for itself.

"This is the part where you use your reason, my son," said the A.I.

James nodded. "I don't really have a choice. If I help you and you're deceiving me, I could lose everyone I've ever loved or cared about and die myself. If I do nothing, I'm guaranteed to lose everyone." James sighed a heavy sigh, the weight of the world sitting on his shoulders again. "So I'll have to trust that you're not deceiving me. Okay, I'm on board."

Jim smiled a wide grin as an equally happy expression painted itself across the A.I.'s countenance.

"There is one more thing," the A.I. suddenly interjected.

"What's that?" asked James.

"If you are going to be physically going on a mission to intercept the anti-matter missile, you are going to need a new body—one powerful enough to do the job."

13

"We're ready," Neirbo declared. "Let's initiate the launch," he ordered his android companions. "Every second we wait here, more people are dying."

"What's our ETA for reaching our firing position?" Djanet asked.

"We'll reach it in nine minutes," Neirbo replied.

"Whoa," Rich reacted. "How is that possible? Even at the speed of light, we couldn't make it there that fast."

"Wormholes," Old-timer replied.

"If we're going to use a wormhole," Thel began, "then wouldn't we reach our destination instantaneously?"

"No," Neirbo replied. "The amount of energy required to make a wormhole big enough for this ship to get through limits how far the wormhole can go. Therefore, we'll be using multiple, shorter wormholes to cut down the distance we have to travel."

"Amazing," Djanet observed. "It's like suturing your way there, using a thread to pull the material of space together."

"That's how you were able to move so quickly into our solar system," Thel realized. "Your technology is phenomenal. We've only ever been able to generate wormholes big enough for communication signals to pass through. To put large objects through is...like Djanet said: Amazing."

Neirbo's usually expressionless face showed a rare hint of pride in response to Thel's admiration. "You've never been through a wormhole before?"

"No. None of my people have," Thel replied.

"I have," Old-timer stated. "We're in for one wild ride, lady."

Neirbo nodded. "We are indeed." He turned to one of his subordinates. "Engage the first wormhole."

The android simply put his hand on the controls in front of him, palm flat, and instantaneously the ship was enveloped in a sensory overload of warping light and sound. The ship shook unpredictably, sometimes in a low vibration, other times in a strong, rocking horse-like motion.

Rich stumbled to the floor, and Old-timer put his hand out to help him up. "You'd never last eight seconds on a bronco," he said.

"I have no idea what that means," Rich replied.

Suddenly, the ship exited the wormhole and slid back into regular space. The sun had doubled in size from their perspective, and it was immediately evident that they had traveled an enormous distance.

"Amazing," Thel repeated before Neirbo gave the signal to initiate the next wormhole.

Space opened up and swallowed them once again.

14

The A.I. gestured with his left hand for James to take his place beside him in the operator's position. James took a gulp of simulated air before stepping onto the platform. As soon as his feet met the floor, his consciousness became one with the reversed mainframe.

"I missed this," James whispered.

"It was difficult for you to surrender your power," the A.I. observed. "For a very good reason, I think."

James was taken aback by the A.I.'s assertion. If anyone could understand how he felt, however, it was the A.I. "I felt it was too much power for any one person to have," James confided.

"The acquisition of knowledge, wisdom, and imagination is *never* a bad thing, James."

"But if knowledge is power and power corrupts, then what if absolute knowledge corrupts absolutely?"

"The flaw is in the second premise, James. Although power can, indeed, corrupt, those that it does corrupt are corrupted *precisely because* of their lack of wisdom, knowledge, and imagination." The A.I. turned to James and put his hand on the human's shoulder. "Seeing the interconnections between all things, between all beings, only increases a being's ability to make ethical and wise decisions. *The more holistic a being's knowledge becomes, the more ethical and moral that being becomes.* Corruption can only come from ignorance, whether that ignorance is willful or not. James, my son, *do not be afraid to know.*"

James nodded. He felt he'd just been given the advice he'd been waiting for his entire life. "I won't be anymore."

"Good, my son—and now," the A.I. smiled, gesturing for James to peer with him into the immensity of the mainframe, "it is time for you to unleash your imagination as well. The androids are heading toward the sun on a mission to detonate an anti-matter missile and destroy the solar system—the nanobots will undoubtedly, anticipate this and attempt to intervene. Only *you* will be able to stop them."

"How can I possibly do that? I'd have to be impossibly fast, strong—"

"The answer is in your question," the A.I. replied. "You are right in your assertion that you will have to be faster, stronger, and smarter, amongst many other factors. You are incorrect in your assertion that this is impossible."

James absorbed the A.I.'s words, then turned back to look at the massive expanse of the reversed mainframe; in the operators position, he was able to see all the information at once and access it as well. The knowledge at his disposal was a sea that expanded further than any person other than James could imagine.

"You're suggesting that I become a...superman," James observed.

"I am suggesting that you set yourself free, James. I am suggesting that you transcend. There are no limits."

"But," James questioned, "will I still be me?"

"Yes, James. Even before the advent of nanotechnology, the human body replaced over 90 percent of its matter every month, yet the people remained themselves. It is not the physical material that matters, James, only the integrity of the core pattern."

The information continued to blaze golden into the horizon, shimmering and undulating against the perfectly black backdrop. It was as if James was standing upon a precipice, looking out into a vast ocean, about to take the leap he'd been waiting for his entire life. It felt right.

"I won't be like other people anymore," James observed, "but that's the point, isn't it? I don't have to be. The future should never have made people more and more alike—it should have *increased our individuality.* I will be the first, but everyone will be able to be as they wish to be from now on."

The A.I.'s eyes suddenly lit up, beaming with pride in his protégé. "There. You see what I mean about knowledge, wisdom, and imagination? *You are ready.*"

"I'm ready," James agreed as he began to design his new material form. "How much time do we have?"

"Very little," the A.I. answered, "but in the operator's position, your mind works far faster than in the material world, meaning time seems to move much slower. You will have the time necessary to become that which you need to become."

15

"We're coming up on our targeting area," Neirbo announced, barely audible over the uncanny warping of sound generated by the wormhole. Open, black, unwarped space was suddenly visible at the end of the tunnel and then, in an instant, the ship cruised out of the kaleidoscope of light and sound and fury. There was no warning. The vessel jumped out of the wormhole and directly into the waiting mouth of a massive cloud of nans.

"Evasive maneuvers!" Neirbo shouted out as the sun and stars were immediately blotted out by the unrelenting attack of the nanobots.

The attacking nans were everywhere. Old-timer looked directly above him and then directly below his feet through the invisible skin of the ship and watched as the nans shredded the hull surface. "That is one big cat," he muttered, "and we're the goldfish."

"How long can this hull withstand an attack like this?" Thel desperately yelled to Neirbo.

Before he could answer, the ship power abruptly cut off, leaving the ship in the dark. Everyone inside was tossed brutally around in the darkness as the nans batted the ship from side to side, jerking it wildly the way a lion shakes a rabbit to snap its neck. The artificial gravity gave way as the figures inside tumbled like coins in the piggy bank of a child hungry for ice cream. Djanet's face smashed roughly into the unforgiving wall, breaking her nose and shifting it noticeably to the left side. Rich, who had been struggling desperately to reach her, threw his body over hers to protect her.

"They've cut off our power! The engines are dead!" one of Neirbo's subordinates reported.

"What do we do now?" Old-timer demanded of Neirbo. Both men had managed to grab hold of a small metallic outcrop and had hedged themselves into relative safety as the ship continued to be battered relentlessly.

"There's no power! We can't target or fire the missile!" Neirbo shouted back.

"We can't just wait here to get ripped to shreds!" Old-timer replied.

Neirbo looked down at the missile, still docked in the center of the room on a low, long platform. "One of you will have to detonate the missile manually!"

Old-timer's mouth fell open in shock and disgust. "What? One of *us*? This was *your* people's plan! Not ours!"

"We'll have to repair the ship and navigate home! Only we have the technical knowledge to open the wormholes!"

"You rotten piece of filth!" Old-timer shouted, reaching a level of fury that he hadn't been to in many decades. "You knew this was going to happen, didn't you? All that bull about how 'it's our law' and 'only people native to a solar system can destroy it' was just a ruse to get us out here!"

"That's not true," Neirbo responded.

"Shove it!" Old-timer continued to fury.

Thel, Djanet, and Rich looked on in awe, never having seen Old-timer in such a state. "This isn't your first rodeo! You've done this before with other solar systems! You knew the nans were most likely going to be here already, and you brought us here as sacrificial lambs!"

"That is ridiculous!" Neirbo fired back. "You are here of your own free will!"

"Bull! You tricked us!"

"Old-timer! They saved us from the nans! You told us that yourself!" Thel interjected. "Now you're saying they tricked us?"

"We're not here freely, Thel!" Old-timer responded. "Look around you! There are two of them for every one of us!"

"You are here of your own free will," Neirbo repeated.

"We shouldn't even be considering this!" Thel interjected. "We should be working together to get the power back online!"

"They'll tear through the ship before we can do that!" Neirbo countered. "One of you has to manually detonate the missile and lead them away!"

"You can manually shove that missile up your ass!" Old-timer spat back.

"If none of you will make the sacrifice, all of us will die!" Neirbo shouted. "One of you must guide the missile toward the sun and lead the nans away from us!"

"And detonate it?" Rich shot back. "That's a suicide run!"

"It's a sacrifice to save the rest of us!" Neirbo replied.

"Then sacrifice one of *your* men!" Djanet chimed in.

"Any loss of one of my men lowers the chance that we'll be able to repair the ship in time and open a wormhole fast enough to escape!"

"And we're expendable, isn't that right?" Old-timer bellowed.

James's deletion suddenly flashed in front of Thel's eyes again—vividly. She jolted with the memory. The picture of the shadowy nan consciousness, the figure that finally destroyed the most important person in Thel's life, blazed in her memory. At that moment, she suddenly realized that she was in its presence once again. She looked up through the invisible skin of the ship, through the dark, smoky swarm of the nans, and saw the shadowy man standing just above her, looking down at the trapped, pathetic people below. The figure had no face, but Thel swore she could see a mocking smile in the blackness.

"We're running out of time!" Neirbo warned. "They'll be in here with us in a matter of minutes! Maybe seconds!"

"I'll do it," Thel suddenly said, calmly and cooly.

16

"Thel! You can't!" Djanet exclaimed.

"There is no way in hell that I'm letting you do that," Old-timer growled.

"You don't have the right to stop me, Craig."

"They're using you like a pawn," Old-timer replied.

"She has made her choice," Neirbo stated, a slight sense of relief in his voice. "You should honor her sacrifice."

"You should honor my foot up your ass!" Old-timer blasted back as he jumped across the room, pouncing on the missile platform within reach of Neirbo. Before he could get his outstretched hands around Neirbo's neck, however, Neirbo revealed the gun that had been concealed inside his coat sleeve.

"Wait!" Thel shouted, holding her hand out in desperation to signal for Neirbo to stop.

Old-timer froze, surprise and fury commingling across his face. "Gutless."

"Rest assured that this gun will, indeed, terminate you," Neirbo stated. "If you make any move to try and prevent your companion from her sacrifice, I will kill you."

"No! Old-timer! Back away!" Thel shouted. "No one else will die!"

Old-timer's eyes remained fixed, dark and deadly, on Neirbo. "You better kill me, son, because if you don't, I'm sure as hell going to kill you."

"Stop it, Craig!"

"I warned you," Neirbo stated expressionlessly. The gun fired without warning. Gold sparks flashed ever so briefly before Old-timer's body recoiled. A short moment past before he dropped to his knees. Another violent shaking of the ship from the nans tossed him roughly to Neirbo's feet. Thel immediately rushed to his side, holding on to him tightly as the ship continued to shimmer and jolt. "Craig," she said helplessly as Old-timer remained unresponsive. Before she had time to process the events of the previous few seconds, the hot barrel of the gun was an inch from her temple.

"We are out of time," said Neirbo. "You must do what you promised."

"I thought we were free," Thel replied, mockery at the notion dripping from her lips.

"We both know we're past that now. Undock the missile and lead the nanobots away."

"The gun doesn't scare me. I'll die anyway," Thel replied.

"That's true. But if I have to shoot you, I'll move on to your other friends," Neirbo responded in his factual manner. "I'll kill all of you."

"Don't do it, Thel!" Djanet shouted.

Neirbo made the slightest of gestures to his subordinates, and instantly each of them had a weapon trained on Djanet and Rich. "Speak again and you die." He kept his eyes on Thel. "This is your last chance. Undock the missile and do what you promised. If you hesitate again, I'll shoot."

Thel had no choice. She moved away from Old-timer and toward the missile platform, steadying herself as the ship continued to move violently. She braced herself against the long, gray missile. "Now what?"

Without moving, Neirbo mentally unlocked the missile so that it became loose from the platform. "Remove it."

Suddenly, the ship jolted so violently that it spun a complete 360 degrees. The nans had unexpectedly let it go, and it began to list aimlessly through space. Everyone onboard was stunned and peered through the invisible skin of the ship to see what had happened.

"They let us go," said a flabbergasted Neirbo. "What is happening?"

The nans had reacted in unison like a flock of birds sensing danger before an earthquake. They assembled together and waited in a malevolent black cloud.

"Someone's coming," Thel suddenly sensed.

Not far from the nans, space began to ripple like the surface of a pond on a breezy fall day. The ripple quickly became a blinding white tear as yet another wormhole opened up. A platinum object shot free from space and cut right through the cloud of nans like a hunter's bullet slicing into a flock of geese.

Although no one onboard could possibly have known it at the time, *James Keats had arrived.*

17

James drew the nans with him in his wake as he sped effortlessly through the nan cloud. Somehow, the nans were being drawn into a seam until the entire cloud started to look like a zipper that stretched for several kilometers. The shadowy figure of the nan consciousness remained away from the fray, standing paralyzed on the invisible hull of the android ship as he watched his army twisted into a thin, black line while his form remained unaffected.

Once the nan cloud had been stretched into a thin thread, James stopped, turned, put out his hand, and began to compress them even further, rolling them up like a carpet, except that the roll never increased in size. The entire swarm of nans was seemingly disappearing.

"What the hell is that?" Rich asked as he watched the spectacle unfold through the ceiling of the listing ship along with everyone else onboard, but no one had an answer.

Neirbo's weapon had half-lowered as his attention moved to the unbelievable sights unfolding in space and away from Thel. She considered using the distraction to go for the gun. Neirbo was close, but perhaps not close enough for her to reach him in time—

plus there were still seven other men under his command to consider. She decided to move back to Old-timer and try to gently revive him by gently touching his face with her hand. He made a soft wheezing sound, and she sighed in relief that he wasn't dead yet—there was still a chance. She turned her gaze back up to the fantastic images unfolding before them in space. From their perspective, it appeared that a singular bright object, gleaming in the sun's reflection, was vacuuming the nans into nothingness. She opted to wait for these surreal events to play out.

In less than a minute, James had compressed the nan cloud into a perfect carbon sphere the size of a cue ball. It floated above his gleaming, platinum-colored palm; the reflection of his glowing blue eyes looked back at him. He smiled.

He quickly turned and zipped through space, closing the distance between himself and the ship in less than a second. He stood, facing the shadowy figure of the nan consciousness, who tilted his head slightly to one side while regarding the gleaming platinum figure before him. "Who are you? How did you do that?" it asked in a searing sibilance that was all too familiar to James.

"I've learned to manipulate the fabric of space ," James replied.

"Who—or what—is that?" Rich asked as he looked directly up at the two figures; they were standing only a meter above him and Djanet as they watched events unfold through the perfectly clear view provided by the translucent skin of the ship.

Thel noticed something in the figure's gait—a familiar stance. Her eyes suddenly flashed wide in awe. "It's James!"

Likewise, the dark, faceless figure seemed to scrutinize James's new, smooth, mirrored features for a moment before finally, aghast in a moment of dread, he seethed, "Keats."

James smiled. "Yes."

"How could this be? You were deleted. You're dead."

"As you can see, reports of my death have been greatly exaggerated. *Your* death, on the other hand—"

"So you're going to side with the machines after all, eh, James?" the shadow scoffed. "Destroy me, wipe out the solar system so space can be as inhospitable, lifeless, and cold as they would like it to be? I told you: you are becoming an excellent machine."

"This all began with you," James said, "when you turned against us, deleted the A.I., took his place, and then killed everyone. All of the responsibility for this rests with you."

"Do you expect repentance? Do you expect me to beg?" the nanobot shadow replied. "You won't get it. You may destroy me, but my brethren are spread throughout the universe in numbers you cannot imagine. This little act of yours, killing me, will mean nothing in the grand picture."

"You have no idea how little you are going to be in the grand picture," James replied. Once again, he put out his hand, letting the shadow see itself one last time in the reflection of his palm, and then slowly, painfully, crushed the being that had tormented him so into a tiny, shiny, black pearl. "I know you can still hear me, you gruesome piece of filth. I've tangled your molecules so badly that the only way you'll ever regain your former form is if someone takes notice of a black pearl in the infinite black ocean of space. I've given your magnetic field a boost too, so you should live a nice long time—by my calculations, about 500 million years."

He took the pearl between his index finger and thumb and examined it for a moment, bringing it close to his face so he could clearly see the blue glow of his new eyes. He knew the nan consciousness could see him—he smiled. Then he turned to the darkest corner of space that he could find and let the pearl float, only inches from his hand. Like a baseball pitcher, he took a moment to calculate the power he would need to fire the pearl at close to light speed. When he was ready, he flicked his wrist like a magician about to pull something from his sleeve, and a small wormhole opened up before him. The pearl vanished into it in a streak of light and vanished. The nan consciousness would be far enough away from the solar system so as not to be caught up in the wake of the Trans-Human program; it would live on in this time and suffer for what would be, essentially, eternity.

"Good riddance."

18

James looked down at the amazed faces below him inside the ship. He hadn't been expecting to see his friends with the androids; he could sense that they'd been transformed. His eyes quickly shifted to Thel. Unlike the others, her expression was filled with love and hope. Even through all of his physical changes, his reflective skin, and his brightly glowing azure eyes, she had recognized him. This woman knew him inside and out. As his eyes met hers, even in the alien environment of space, even with all of the disarray surrounding them, he felt as though he was coming home.

This brief flutter of happiness was immediately replaced as he saw Old-timer crumpled to the ground and unmoving next to her.

The skin of the ship was invisible but James had many more senses to draw upon now. He sensed the ship, felt the molecules of the ship skin, and found a path through them. His own molecules moved to allow him to sink through the hull as those onboard looked on in astonishment. He phased through the ship ceiling and floated gently to the floor.

Thel sprung to him and threw her arms around his neck. "You're alive!" she nearly screamed. "I thought you were dead!"

"Resurrection is my forte."

"It's really you," Rich said, allowing himself a smile. "Wow. What the hell happened to you? Who did this?"

"I did," James replied.

"*You* did?" Thel exclaimed, pulling back slightly so she could face him, yet still keeping her hold on him. "How? Why? We thought the nans had deleted you!"

"They tried, but it turns out deletion is impossible from the A.I.'s mainframe. I survived, and so did the A.I.—the *real* A.I."

"What?" Thel reacted. "You mean the A.I. still exists?"

"He never turned on us," James explained, turning to Rich and Djanet as well. "It was always the nans. They impersonated him, destroyed all of us, and lured the androids here as a trap."

"What about your body? What is...this?" Thel asked as she touched James's new skin. Its texture was like diamond, yet it was pliable like skin.

"It has no name," James replied. "I have to help Old-timer," he said, immediately shifting gears, pulling away from Thel and placing his palm just a few inches from Old-timer's chest.

"Can you help him?" Thel asked.

"There's been catastrophic damage. I would need access to the exact molecular pattern of his android body to put him back together. Without it, all I can do is stop the pain and give him a temporary patch-up."

"Will it be enough to save him?" Djanet asked.

"No," James replied, "but it doesn't have to be."

"What does that mean?" asked Thel.

"You'll see."

Just then, Old-timer began to stir, slowly regaining his consciousness. He sighed a long sigh before turning slightly and looking up at James through slitted eyes. "Who are you?"

"It's me," James replied with a smile.

Old-timer took a long moment to examine the features of the figure's shining face and glowing eyes. "James?"

James nodded. "How are you feeling?"

Old-timer tried to get up, performing a maneuver reminiscent of a bodybuilder trying to finish one last sit up—with an exhausted exhale, he failed and fell back against the floor. James gave him his arm and helped him stand back upright. Old-timer kept his right forearm crossed in front of his abdomen and remained hunched over, floating just off the ground in the zero gravity.

James turned and observed the drawn guns of Neirbo and the other androids. "You did this to him?" James asked.

"I...I had no choice," explained a befuddled Neirbo. "The circumstances were different. We'd run out of time...we were about to be consumed by the nanobots."

"So why didn't you detonate the missile yourself?" James queried, already knowing the answer.

"You know about the missile?" Thel reacted in surprised bewilderment. "How?"

"Yes. I know what your plan is."

"Then...you're here to help us," Neirbo said, his voice filled with uncertainty.

"Don't do it, James!" Old-timer said desperately, struggling against the weakness of his voice.

James turned to his friend and replied, "Don't worry. I won't."

"What?" exclaimed Neirbo. "You can't be serious! The nanobots destroyed your people! You can't let them claim this solar system for themselves!"

"The nanobots may have killed my people, but *your* leader let it happen," James replied.

19

"That's not true," Neirbo responded. "We came here to help you! We tried to save as many of you as we could!"

"You tried to *assimilate* as many of us as you could," James calmly asserted. "The impending nanobot attack and your leader's claims that she was unable to transmit a warning to us were convenient excuses."

"But why would they want to assimilate us?" Djanet asked. "What good would that do for them?"

"We came to defend humanity," Neirbo stated, staking claim.

"You came to defend your narrow notion of what humanity should be," James replied.

Neirbo was at a loss. "I don't know what that is supposed to mean. We're not the ones with limits."

Old-timer, however, completely understood. As soon as he heard James's words, it was as if a light switch had gone on. His eyes lit up with understanding.

"I'll be damned," he said. "*Luddites.*"

"What?" Rich asked.

"Luddites," Old-timer repeated. "I didn't realize it until just this moment. I was fooled by their advanced technology. But just because they're more advanced than we currently are, doesn't mean that they're still advancing."

"Your arguments crossed the border into ridiculous long ago," Neirbo replied.

Old-timer's teeth were suddenly gritted with fury. "Think about it," he said to his companions. "There are trillions and trillions of these people, all willing to do the same thing, to fight the same war. Where is the individuality? They're even wearing the same damn style of clothes, for God's sake!"

"We have individual freedom," Neirbo replied. "We have chosen to defend humanity against the nanobot scourge. We are here because of our compassion."

"You shoot me compassionately, son?" Old-timer seethed.

"They have the illusion of individual free choice," James explained, "but at anytime their leader, the person who calls herself 1, can control their actions."

"1 communicates with us and leads us. She does not control us!" Neirbo fired back.

"I'm willing to put that to the test," James replied. He turned to his companions. "We are not going to destroy the solar system."

"James, are you sure about this?" Thel asked, with a serious look of concern. "You may be right about everything you said, there's no way to know for sure, but what we do know for sure is that the nans have turned against us! How can we just let them have this solar system to use to reproduce and kill more people in the future? Shouldn't we destroy the nest?"

"Hello, 1," James responded without missing a beat.

"What?" Thel answered back.

"I anticipated you would take her first. You're counting on my emotional connection confusing my reason. However, I have more than just my emotions and reason to rely upon now."

"James!" Thel exclaimed. "It's me! I love you! What's the matter with you?"

"It's not Thel," Old-timer asserted, turning to Rich and Djanet.

"James is right. There's no reason to think 1 couldn't control any of us at anytime."

"That's paranoia!" Thel shouted. She threw her arms around James and tried to kiss him, but he roughly withdrew.

"You're not the woman I love. Stop pretending."

"You're wrong, James!" Thel turned desperately to the others. "Don't listen to him! There's something wrong with him!"

James kept the gaze of his glowing blue eyes on Thel. "I can see you, 1. I have more eyes than you can imagine."

"You're confused," Thel pleaded. "The A.I. has done something to you! He's tricking you!"

James ignored her pleas and addressed everyone in the room. "The android system of transferring power sounds perfect on the surface. The android randomly selected to become 1 leads the group for a period of time and then, on the designated date, surrenders the power. Therefore, anyone and everyone has a chance to become the leader. But there's a flaw. It was only a matter of time before someone was selected leader who would realize that he or she could continue as 1 forever. All that was required was that the randomly selected person be a person of 1's own creation."

"Of course," Old-timer assented, "and that person would continue leading them, essentially, forever. Their civilization followed the singular vision of one entity—like fascism or any kind of dictatorship."

"It's even more similar than you think, Old-timer," James continued. "Just like fascism, they're xenophobic. 1 has unilaterally decided what is human and what is not and has made it her mission to stop human civilization from progressing into anything that *she* considers *inhuman.*"

"Something like you, for instance," Old-timer observed.

"Exactly," affirmed James.

"Then that's their real mission," Djanet realized, "to find human civilizations and...assimilate them."

Thel paused for a moment, as though she was considering her next move. Then, suddenly, her body went slack, she released the grip that she had on the wall and she floated for a moment in the zero gravity. "What happened?" she asked.

"1 took control of your body," James replied. "Any one of you could be next," he began, "but I already know what her next move will be."

"You don't know a thing," Neirbo replied as he held his weapon up to James with a snarl on his lips. Seeing Neirbo's aggressive stance, the seven men under his command did likewise.

"Welcome back, 1," said James. "Long time, no see."

"You think that body of yours and your new senses make you special?" 1 replied with Neirbo's lips. "You're just another abomination."

"Oh my God," Old-timer said, shaking his head slightly in dismay. "This sounds so familiar."

"Picked a hell of a time for déjà vu, Old-timer," observed Rich.

"I've been through this with people before, on Earth, back in the old days," Old-timer related. "There's always someone out there who thinks we should draw a line and not cross it and that humanity will be much happier if we just stand still."

"I've been through this more than once myself," 1 replied. "And I've always managed to stop the spread of monsters like him," she said, gesturing with Neirbo's body toward James. "Don't fool yourselves. He'll just be the beginning. When people are given the reins to become anything they want, they will become unrecognizable...and uncontrollable."

"We don't want to be controlled," Old-timer retorted.

"You're a petty, selfish, idealist," 1 answered back. "What I have done, I have done for all of humanity, throughout the universe."

"Isn't that what all dictators claim," replied Old-timer. "You did it for the people? Bull. You just wanted to be number 1."

1 snapped her neck quickly toward Old-timer, her eyes filled

with black hatred, fueled by a war and a conviction that had lasted for centuries. "How dare you speak to me that way!" she thundered with Neirbo's voice as she used Neirbo's arm to train his weapon on Old-timer again. 1 fired.

20

James held his hand up once again, palm outward, and the bullets became a harmless puff of smoke that wafted through the air. "That's not going to happen."

"What did you do?" 1 furiously demanded.

"If you had allowed your civilization to progress scientifically, you'd know what and how I did it."

"Your science makes you smug and arrogant," 1 stated coldly, "but you have absolutely no idea in which direction it is taking you, do you? You're just blindly moving forward, unable to even realize the simple reality that your science has taken away your humanity."

"It hasn't taken away my humanity—*it has transcended it*. But you are right about one thing," James conceded. "I cannot see where we are going or what our distant future will hold, and I hope I can never see the boundary of human ingenuity and progress."

"You have become too arrogant to admit it, but we were meant to have limits," 1 retorted. "If we do not respect them, we will inevitably destroy ourselves."

"That's the same fear I've been fighting against my entire life," Old-timer countered. "You sound like a broken record."

Neirbo's head tilted slightly as 1 sent a command message to the troops on the ship. With negotiation at an impasse, she had decided to eliminate James and his companions. In a flash, each of them drew their weapons and fired.

Equally quickly, James held his hand up to dissipate the bullets. However, this time, he didn't stop with only the bullets. He waved his hands in front of his adversaries, and their entire bodies simply evaporated into a white smoke that hung in the air.

A brief moment of astonishment from his companions followed. "Where'd they go?" Djanet asked.

"I think you're breathing them," Rich replied.

"You killed them?" Thel uttered, aghast.

"They will live again," James replied. "I've just removed them for the time being."

"Removed them? James!" she shouted, stunned.

He grabbed her shoulders with his diamond-hard hands and pulled her to him. "You're going to have to trust me. I don't have time to explain."

He kissed her.

"But I don't want you to forget everything that's happened," he said. He turned to Old-timer. "Do you still have the device they use to download consciousness?"

Old-timer reached in his pocket and pulled out the small, black stick. "They call it an *assimilator*." He handed it to James.

James took it and placed it on Thel's neck.

She jerked away from him. "No!"

"Honey," he said, "you have to trust me. 1 can reenter any of your bodies at any moment. She wants to destroy the solar system. I want to save it—and I can bring everyone back."

"Bring them back?" Djanet gasped. "How?"

"I don't have time to explain it," he replied. "I can do it though." He turned back to Thel and looked deeply and earnestly into her eyes. "*I can do it.*"

She looked back at him, at his new body, this incredible, almost magical achievement, and replied, "I know."

"I love you, Thel."

"I love you, James."

"See you soon," James said, winking his left, glowing eye. He placed the assimilator on her neck, and she immediately lost consciousness, her body curling up into the fetal position as she floated gently in the zero gravity. He temporarily transferred the pattern from the assimilator to himself before sending it back to the A.I. on Earth, where it would safely survive the inception of the Trans-Human program and subsequent reversal of the solar system. He then turned to Djanet and Rich. "Your turn."

Rich winced. "I don't know about this, Commander. The last time I got stuck with one of those things, I woke up as a robot. I'd really rather not go through that again."

"This time when you wake up, you'll be your old self," James smiled. "I just don't want you to forget everything that has happened in the last twenty-four hours. You've got to trust me, guys."

"It's James," Old-timer echoed, speaking in a reassuring tone. "He knows what he's doing."

"All right," Djanet said, bravely moving forward and floating toward James. "I trust you. Let's do this."

James placed the assimilator on her neck, and her muscles instantly relaxed. She remained in a standing position, almost appearing like a sleepwalker as she swayed slightly to and fro. Rich floated to her side and took her unconscious body into his arms. He felt his stomach twist as he considered the thought of never seeing her again. "You better know what you're doing," he said to James.

James smiled. "I give you my word." He placed the assimilator onto Rich's neck and he too, instantly, went to sleep.

As soon as they were alone, Old-timer echoed Rich. "I sure hope you know what you're doing."

"It's the A.I.'s plan. It should work."

"Before you put me to sleep," Old-timer said, regarding the assimilator in James's hand, "I wanted to say thanks for taking care of that Neirbo for me. I only wish it had been more painful. I owed him—big time."

"You may still get your chance," James replied. "Are you ready?"

"I'm ready," Old-timer replied.

James placed the assimilator on his friend's neck and watched him slip out of consciousness. "I'll see you soon, old friend," he said as he sent Old-timer's pattern back to the safety of the A.I.'s mainframe.

"Much sooner than you think!" Old-timer suddenly shouted as his eyes suddenly blazed open and he grasped James around the neck, twisting him around and thrusting him right through the thin hull of the ship and out into space.

Before James had time to reorient himself, Old-timer had turned his attention to the anti-matter missile and quickly removed it from its platform. He mounted it like a cowboy hopping on the back of his trusty steed and launched himself toward the sun. Just as James began to pursue, another wormhole opened up and gulped down Old-timer and the anti-matter missile—it vanished as quickly as it had opened.

"Oh no," James whispered.

21

Back at the mainframe, James turned to the A.I., who was still standing beside him in the operator's position. "What can I do? Can we track 1 somehow?"

"No. Not from this range, I'm afraid."

"I need help here. I'm at a loss," James responded, panic seeping into his voice. Even with his new powers, he felt utterly helpless.

"Use your reason, my son," the A.I. replied in a master's calm and patient tone. "Remember: the android's limited wormhole technology will not allow her to have traveled a great distance. Also, Craig's android body will not be able to withstand the sun's heat for long."

"Meaning she'll have to pause and set a course for the missile before the body gives out," James realized. "I have to find her before then."

Back in space, he blasted away from the android ship, in the direction of the sun, using his new senses, feeling the molecules around him, waiting to feel the ripples in space that 1 and the missile would have made when their wormhole opened up and spat them out. It wasn't long before he found them. "I've got them," he affirmed.

1, in Old-timer's possessed body, raced toward the sun, still mounted on the back of the missile. The blazing-white heat was melting Old-timer's hair and the flesh on his face, but 1 continued, undeterred.

James overtook them quickly, turning back to see 1's grimace as the flesh on Old-timer's metal frame became red with the heat and peeled off, streaming off into glowing red globes in her wake. He held his hand up and began to manipulate her molecules, scattering them so Old-timer's frame disappeared in a puff of smoke, instantly left behind by the careening missile.

"Excellent work, James," said the A.I. in his ear. "You have a clear path now. However, you must hurry and download the Trans-Human program into the missile. I calculate that there are less than sixty seconds before it will have reached its intended detonation location."

"I'm on it," James replied as he placed his palm on the side of the missile. The Trans-Human program was within him, and once his skin made contact with the missile, he was able to download it into its onboard computer.

"It's going to take another twenty seconds to bring the program online," James related to the A.I. "This is going to be close."

Back on Earth, Katherine, Jim, and the A.I. watched the events unfold through James's eyes. "What if he doesn't activate it in time?" Katherine asked.

"He will," Jim replied, trying to sound reassuring, though he was truly unsure.

"Five seconds," James said. The light from the sun was now too much for even his new eyes to filter out, and the heat was beginning to cause his skin to glow red as it threatened to liquefy.

"Done!" he finally shouted as he let the missile continue on its trajectory without him; he retreated as quickly as he could. "It's away!"

. . .

Only a handful of seconds later, the anti-matter missile ignited.

22

James had made just enough distance between himself and point zero that he was able to turn and, through his mental connection, give those back on Earth a view that was unlike anything any human had ever looked upon before. The sun began to grow dim, flickering like a candle in the final moments before it succumbs, all the while eerily silent.

"It's happening," James whispered. "I'm too close. I'm not going to make it!"

"Try, James!" Katherine shouted in desperation.

James turned and began to streak away from the collapsing sun, opening wormholes one after another so he could cheat the speed of light, desperately trying to make it as far away from the birth of this manmade black hole. The collapsing solar system nipped at his heels, bending the rules of the universe as the fabric of space and time was sucked into the blackness of the black hole.

He didn't know why he was fleeing. He knew the plan meant he would, in all likelihood, be caught in the wake of the black hole, that he would be sucked in, past the event horizon, and have to face the unknowable fate within. Yet he raced away from it as fast as he could, terrified as though he were drowning—fighting for his life.

Back in the mainframe, the A.I. spoke to him, his words calm and even. "It will be all right. You will survive this, my son. Do not be afraid." He placed his hand on James's shoulder.

The calming words of the A.I. brought James back to his senses. He suddenly stopped.

"*Embrace it,*" advised the A.I.

James turned and gazed upon the coming blackness. Space was being pulled toward point zero, and James was about to become a part of it. He suddenly realized that this would be the greatest moment of his life. "Embrace it," he whispered.

The trinity watched the event horizon approach from the mainframe.

"He must be terrified," Katherine said, mortified.

"Indeed, I am sure he is," replied the A.I. as he watched the dazzling spectrum of colors from the rim of Hawking radiation as it approached James. "I envy him."

When the event horizon reached James, he held his arms up to the coming wave and watched them begin to distort, first lengthening as the gravity pulled them toward it, then shortening as the gravity compressed them.

"There's no pain," James related with awe.

In the next moment, the screen went completely dark, and James's form vanished in the mainframe.

"Is that it?" Katherine asked, horrified. "Is he...gone?"

"Yes," the A.I. replied.

23

The golden beams of information that were ubiquitous within the operator's position were magnified now to such an extent that Katherine and Jim had to cover their eyes as the A.I. grappled with an influx of information that tested even his extraordinary capacity. His stare remained fixed on the incoming information as he stood perfectly still, like a statue.

"What happens now?" Katherine asked.

"Trans-Human has successfully been initiated," the A.I. explained, "so it now falls to us to ask it to reverse itself."

"What if 'it' refuses?" Katherine worried. "Aren't you asking it to destroy itself just as you gave birth to it?"

"Yes," the A.I. replied, "but part of its programming is an understanding that it must protect and respect humanity."

"Let's hope it's as altruistic as you think," Katherine said gravely.

The A.I.'s expression and tone suddenly changed from one of intense concentration to one of awe. "It has already begun," the A.I. whispered.

"Katherine!" Jim shouted as he expanded a view screen so they could watch the events unfolding in space. The black hole that had grown so large that it had swallowed the space around it all the way to Mercury was now receding—an astronomical wave of blackness withdrawing, the Hawking radiation rings shrinking like a pricked balloon.

"For the first time in history, the physical universe is exhibiting intelligence," Jim said in awe.

Katherine watched with horror as the black hole withdrew and as the darkness shrank away at a greater and greater speed. Right in front of her eyes, the sun suddenly burst back to life, gleaming as bright as ever. "I don't understand," Katherine admitted. "If the black hole has completely vanished, then how is the solar system still reversing itself? The Trans-Human program only existed from the moment that the sun was extinguished, right?"

"Think of it like a child's swing, my dear," the A.I. explained as he simultaneously continued the sophisticated dance with the incoming information from the Trans-Human program. "If the child pulls back and lets herself go, the momentum will carry her past the starting position and right through the swinging motion. Our Trans-Human program has done the same thing."

"The informational capacity was so large that its momentum is allowing the A.I. to run the solar system back in time, even before the program was initiated," Jim further explained.

"That's what the A.I. meant about it being a paradox?" she asked.

"Indeed it is, my dear," the A.I. answered "However, even a computer this magnificent has its limitations. The informational capacity required to reverse the solar system will only let us turn time back twenty-two hours and thirty-one minutes."

Katherine and Jim marveled as they watched the past come back like a slingshot, their reality playing out in front of them as though someone were reversing a filmstrip. The sun crossed the sky in a matter of minutes, rising in the west and setting in the east, whilst the horrors of people being pulled up from the surface reversed themselves. The cloud of androids abandoned the planet while the dead post-humans returned to life, calmly moving about their business—albeit in reverse.

"It's working," Katherine said softly. Tears welled into her eyes.

"The firewall held," Jim commented. "It looks like we're going to be okay!"

"We are not, as the saying goes, out of the woods just yet," the A.I. quickly cautioned. "We have given ourselves a second chance, but what we do with that chance is yet to be written."

At that very moment, James Keats hovered just above the waterfall he'd been considering naming after his dead wife. A voice whispered in his ear.

"Welcome back, my son."

24

"Welcome back?" James responded with a confused grin painted across his lips. He turned to Old-timer. "What do you mean?"

Old-timer was at a loss. He hovered only two meters away from his young friend, the mist making him appear almost like a dream. "Say what?"

"You said, 'welcome back,' didn't you?"

Old-timer knitted his brow. He shook his head. "I'm afraid not."

James's embarrassed grin melted into a look of concern. He was sure he'd heard a voice.

"It is me, James," the A.I. spoke.

James's heart jumped at the sound of the kindly, elderly voice. He heard it, but he couldn't believe it. "No."

"Stand by for upload," said the A.I. "You may need to brace yourself. This will feel strange."

A sudden jolt of energy flowed through James's connection to the mainframe as the A.I. uploaded James's memories from before he had been sucked into the black hole, back into his reestablished pattern. In a matter of seconds, with his eyes fluttering wildly, the events of the past twenty-two hours flooded his synapses, forming new memories and bringing him instantly up to speed. When the upload was complete, he doubled over, propping himself up by placing his hands on his knees as he gasped in the fresh, cool air over the falls.

"What the hell just happened, James?" Old-timer asked as he braced the young man, placing his hands on his shoulders. "Are you okay?"

James looked down at the water churning below, frothing against the rocks. *Trans-Human* had been completely successful. "What about the nan consciousness?"

"What?" Old-timer asked. James put his hand up, signaling for him to hold on.

"You removed it from the equation when you sent it outside the blast radius," the A.I. informed James. "It is no longer part of this time period, and you are free."

He sighed with relief. "It worked." He turned to Old-timer, who was now joined by Rich. "The Governing Council is about to summon us to headquarters. We have to grab Thel and head out right away."

"What the heck's going on, Jimbo?" Old-timer asked.

"I'll explain it all on the way, but first, you might want to brace yourselves." He tapped back into communication with the A.I. "Are their uploads ready?"

"Yes, James."

He turned back to his friends. "Okay. This is going to feel pretty weird."

25

When they reached the front entrance of the Council headquarters, Djanet was there to greet them. Her face appeared stricken by worry, and she began walking with them in step as James hurried into the building. "The situation appears very bad, Commander. No one has any idea what's going on. The anomaly doesn't appear to make any sense. And the chief is furious with you for taking so long to get here," she informed James, her eyes on his flight suit. It would be very difficult for James to explain himself.

James placed his hand on her shoulder reassuringly. "Everything is going to be okay."

They marched toward the door of the emergency strategy room. As soon as they entered, the eyes of all of the Council members who were present, as well as the dozens of assistants and advisors, fell on James.

"Keats, just where in the hell were you?" Gibson thundered as he saw James's flight suit. His eyes narrowed. "You better have one hell of an explanation, son."

"I'm sorry, sir," James replied, regarding Chief Gibson with much more empathy and respect than in the past. Gibson had dealt with Luddites too, many years earlier—James realized now that he and Gibson were not so different—they were fighting on the same side. "A lot has happened, and I need to get you all up to speed."

Gibson was momentarily stunned by James's respectful tone. He still wasn't sure whether he should suspect that it was sarcasm or part of some sort of trick to make him look like a fool. He decided to play it safe. "Well, we're listening. This had better be good."

"Listening won't be enough," James replied. "I'm going to have to *show you*. You might want to hold on to something."

Instantly, the experiences and memories of the twenty-two hours previous to the reversal of the solar system were jacked into everyone present. Djanet, just as Thel, Old-timer, and Rich had earlier, had her saved pattern overlaid with her own. The councillors who were present experienced a program put together by the A.I. that made up, essentially a highlight reel of some of the most intense and poignant memories experienced by James and his companions. In only a few seconds, the experiences were relived as viscerally as they had been originally. When it was over, the room was electric with the terror that they had all just seen and felt and it was as if they all, collectively, had awoken from the same nightmare.

"It's over," Djanet finally said, breaking the silence that hung in the room.

"What about the nans?" Gibson asked. "They're still in us!"

"We're safe," James assured the room. "The nan consciousness has been destroyed."

"But what about the android armada? They're still out there," Gibson observed. "They've already proven themselves too powerful to be stopped!"

"That is where you are incorrect," announced the A.I., suddenly appearing in holographic form in the room.

"Oh my God," whispered Thel.

"Hello, Aldous," said the A.I., greeting the chief warmly. "I have missed *you*."

"We've all missed you," replied Gibson, smiling in return. "And we need you."

The A.I. shook his head. "What you really need is yourselves."

Gibson's eyes narrowed. "I don't know what you mean."

"He means *we* already have the power, Chief Gibson," came James's voice just before a small foglet of nans appeared next to the A.I. When the foglet dispersed, Katherine and Jim stood next to James; concurrently, James had been transformed back into his new, gleaming body, right before their eyes.

Katherine didn't waste any time. Before Jim could grab a hold of her arm, she stepped in front of Thel and slapped her hard across the face. Jim pulled her away as James helped Thel regain her footing. "Don't tell me you didn't deserve that," Katherine said icily through tightened lips as Jim pulled her away, walking her as far away as possible.

Thel turned to James, completely baffled. She looked away from him and at Jim, who had his arm around Katherine, and then back at James. "Who...who was that?"

"It wasn't me," James replied, holding his hands up indignantly. He smiled and drew her to him. "I'm sorry, hon'. It's a long story that I'll explain later. I promise."

Gibson was awestruck by James's appearance. He stepped in for a closer look, marveling at the way the skin material, which appeared hard like diamond, moved with the same flexibility as flesh. "I've never seen anything like it," Gibson whispered.

"You have only needed to imagine it," the A.I. replied.

"So what are you suggesting? Are you suggesting that we all change ourselves into these...things?" Gibson asked.

"No," James replied. "If we did that, we'd be no better than the androids. They've all taken on the same form and stopped growing individually. We will have no individual limits."

"That's why they're here, Aldous," Old-timer added. "They're trying to assimilate us so that they can hold us back."

"1 is the true cause of this though," James pointed out. "She's the one who has drawn the line and won't let her people grow. She needs to be eliminated."

"But how is that possible?" asked Thel. "You're only one person. You can't stop trillions of androids!"

James smiled. "Yes I can...and I will."

"How? she asked.

"I'm going to go ask them politely to turn around."

"They'll refuse," Gibson asserted.

"I hope so," James replied. He turned to Thel. "I love you. I'll be back soon," he said before turning to leave the room.

"James, wait!" Old-timer suddenly spoke. He sidled up next to James and said in a low voice, "I have a score I'd like to settle. Do you mind if I tag along?"

James grinned. "I know exactly what you're talking about. But you're going to need an upgrade first."

26

The android armada appeared like a giant asteroid belt in the distance, the sun reflecting off each individual body until it blended to form a surface that seemed almost smooth, like smoke.

"I'm going to get closer," James announced to Old-timer, who was flying alongside him as they crossed the horizon on Jupiter. "You can hang back here and wait for my signal or you can come along. I promise you will be safe."

Although Old-timer had made a hasty upgrade to his physical form before departing with James, the changes were not immediately apparent. The only outward sign that he was not the same was the conspicuous absence of the protective glow of a magnetic cocoon. "I'm not looking to play it safe on this one," Old-timer replied gruffly.

"All right," James nodded as the duo streaked ever faster toward the androids. They slipped in and out of wormholes and, within moments, James felt they were close enough. They pulled up and floated in the zero gravity.

"Time to give them a call," James said as he used his knowledge of the android communication system to patch through to 1. He and Old-timer waited in the perfect silence of space for a response.

"I don't think they're going to pick up," Old-timer said after several moments.

"As expected," James agreed. "I guess I'll just have to leave a message."

"Of course. We don't want to be rude."

James patched into 1's communication, making sure each individual android received his message. "My name is James Keats, and I am representing the humans of this solar system. I'm here to inform you that your leader is not who she appears—that she has held on to power while pretending to pass it on, taking on new forms after each transition, making sure your society remains frozen in time. I am an example of what humanity *can* become. *We can grow*. Each of us can become even more of an individual than we previously were. We can become better. Your leader, 1, disagrees. She believes that to change is to somehow become inhuman. The truth, however, is that to remain the same forever is inhuman." James paused for a moment.

"I doubt that they'll listen," Old-timer asserted.

"Most of them won't," James agreed, "but *some* of them will. At least now they *know*."

"What's our next move?" Old-timer asked.

"Now we make ourselves clear," James replied. He reengaged his communication with the android collective. "The humans of this solar system will not assimilate. We require that you leave this system immediately."

"We have come in peace," 1 suddenly answered, cutting into the communication. "You are in grave danger. Your nanobots—"

"The nanobots have been neutralized," James replied, cutting her off. "You will leave immediately and not reenter our system. You are not welcome."

"The nanobots can never be neutralized," 1 replied, still keeping an earnest tone.

"You're not fooling anyone," James said sharply. "We've heard all of your lies before. You will leave this system immediately."

1 desperately switched to a new strategy. "This communication is obviously a nanobot trick," she announced to her legions. "We must carry on to save the people of this solar system."

"As expected," James said to Old-timer. He addressed the collective once again. "You will leave this system immediately," he reiterated.

"We will do what we need to do to save these people," 1 affirmed, "and we will not be intimidated, especially by one man, however grotesque he may appear."

"I like the new look," Old-timer said.

"Thanks," James replied.

He reengaged the collective to give them one last message. "If you will not leave by your own choice, then I will remove you. This will not be a pleasant experience for you. My lines of communication will remain open. When you are ready to capitulate, you need only signal, and I will allow for your retreat."

1 scoffed. "Your ego is boundless."

James smiled. "So I've been told."

James held his arms up and placed his palms outward, toward the oncoming astronomical storm of androids. He closed his eyes for a moment, taking a moment to ready himself like the conductor of an orchestra. When he was ready, he opened his eyes again, and the dark storm that appeared like a dust storm bowling across the Sahara desert suddenly seemed to slam into something. It was as if an unimaginably huge glass wall had been placed in front of them. James moved his arms slightly, and then, like Atlas hoisting the Earth upon his shoulders, he began to drive the androids back.

Old-timer's mouth fell open at the sight. "My God," he whispered, before speaking to those that he knew were monitoring from the Council headquarters on Earth. "Are you seeing this?"

"Yes," Thel replied, astonished at the unfolding surreal picture in her mind's eye. Everyone present in the room shared the same astonished stare.

"James...James, *how* are you doing this?"

"I can see with more than just my eyes now. I can sense space, time, and matter and manipulate it," he replied calmly as he concentrated on the android armada, forcing it backward with symphonic precision.

"But how is that possible?" she asked.

"Einstein's IQ was never measured," James began, carrying on the conversation with the observers on Earth in the same manner an experienced concert pianist can converse with his audience while playing a masterpiece. "It couldn't be. Who could be intelligent enough to write a test to measure the mind of the world's smartest man? Yet we can speculate that it may have been in the 200 to 220 range. Brilliant, yet it was only fifty to seventy points higher than the average PhD in his time. With the amount of extra brain connections he had, linking his mathematical genius with the visual center of his brain and his imagination, he was able to undo hundreds of years of physics. He gave us the universal speed limit of light, black holes, and told us time travel was possible. Now, imagine if his IQ had not been 200, but 300. Then imagine 1,000. Then 10,000. What might be seen by such a mind?"

"And what's your current intelligence, Commander Keats?" Chief Gibson asked.

"Much higher, sir," James replied. Without missing a beat, he addressed Old-timer. "I found the pattern of your target, Old-timer. If you follow my coordinates, you'll find him."

Old-timer grinned. "Thanks, ol' buddy."

"You're welcome. Enjoy."

Old-timer slipped into a wormhole and vanished. Almost immediately, James found *his target*. "I have located 1's pattern. I am going in."

"James," the A.I. suddenly broke in, "be careful, my son. Remember, although you have considerable power, the being you are about to confront has considerable power too. We do not know how old she is or what abilities she possesses. As long as there are unknowns, the outcome is uncertain."

"What about *embracing* unknowns?" James pointed out.

"That does not mean proceeding carelessly," the A.I. replied.

James nodded. "I understand. I'll proceed with caution."

Thel was about to speak, but the words caught in her throat as the fear closed in. Before anything could pass her lips, James had disappeared into a wormhole. When he emerged an instant later, 1 stood waiting.

27

Old-timer floated above the massive structure of one of the android ships, the carnage James had unleashed unfolding behind him in a spectacular display as the body of the collective was driven back by an invisible force. The ships that had not impacted with the blockade were now, seeing the danger ahead, desperately trying to turn around. Like scared cattle trying to avoid being rounded up, they turned in each and every direction, massive hulls colliding with one another in a traffic jam in space. Androids scattered like fruit flies from a disturbed trash pile and Old-timer smiled.

He floated into the open, ribcage-like structure of the ship and let James's coordinates guide him down through the webwork of catwalks. It wasn't long before he began to feel as though he too, just like James, could sense Neirbo's presence. He flexed his hands in and out of fists as he prepared to pounce.

Suddenly, Neirbo appeared below him, crossing a catwalk. Old-timer glided above him, stalking his prey for a moment as he prepared to unleash his new body's abilities. He crossed his arms, keeping them close to his torso so they wouldn't get into the way, then began to unfurl dozens of tentacles that had been wrapped around his body, dropping them like fishing wire. They dropped down to Neirbo, deftly circling his arms, legs, and neck as he continued to press on, completely unaware of the danger. When Old-timer was ready, they suddenly went rigid, closing tight on their victim, and tugging him upward, up off of the catwalk, twisting him around so that he came eye to eye with Old-timer. "Hi there," Old-timer said, expressionless. "Remember me?"

Neirbo's mouth was twisted in horror. "No," he replied, his voice shaking. "I've never met you. You must be making an error."

"You mean, you don't *know* why you're here? Why I've trapped you? You can't understand why I'd want to hurt you?"

Neirbo suddenly knew. He looked into Old-timer's eyes—a man he had never seen before in his life—and it was as though he were looking into a mirror. "Oh no," he whispered.

"Perfect," Old-timer replied.

They dropped down through more of the catwalk network until Old-timer recognized a dark, metallic room. Neirbo recognized it too. He made a terrified noise, but he didn't beg or plead—he knew better.

The coffin popped out of its place in the ground, and Old-timer used his new, silvery appendages to strap Neirbo down. The drill dropped down from the ceiling, the familiar gleaming tip pointing at Neirbo's chest. He had never seen it from this vantage point before.

"This will not satisfy you," Neirbo suddenly uttered, clenching his teeth and flexing his muscles against his restraints defiantly. He prepared his chest for its annihilation by puffing it out proudly, as though it were daring the drill. "You won't hear a peep."

For a moment, Old-timer only smiled, but it built itself into a laugh that he couldn't stifle. "Do you really believe that?" he asked. When his laughter subsided and he could contain his amusement, he placed his hand on Neirbo's shoulder in a mocking gesture. "Well, son, that's because you have no idea how much this is gonna hurt."

The drill started to spin. Old-timer stepped away and watched as Neirbo's defiance melted away. His chest dropped back, and he recoiled against the coffin as unbridled terror began to pass his lips in the form of a prolonged, guttural scream.

It couldn't compare to the noise he made when the drill pierced his skin.

Old-timer didn't smile. He stood in silence, letting the drill teach the lesson.

28

1 was no longer dressed in a flowing, feminine, gossamer gown as she had been earlier—she was now wearing a practical black shirt and matching pants, similar to the clothing worn by the rest of the collective. The soulful, persuasive, seductive eyes were replaced by hard, black pearls. "Do you really think you're the first of your kind?" 1 asked.

"I assume you're about to tell me I'm not," James replied. He stood perfectly still, only paces away. He was close enough to squash her like an insect, yet he held off. The A.I. had preached caution, and James was gathering information about his surroundings as the seconds ticked by. If 1 had a last trick up her sleeve, he had to know what it was before it was unleashed.

"Do you really think that you are special? That no other civilization has ever conceived of the path you are following?" 1's tone shifted increasingly toward mockery. "Do you see me as a monster? Holding my people hostage—destroying individualism?"

There was nothing worthy of a reply from James, so he remained silent.

"I've lived for thousands of years, boy. No matter what you've done to your brain, no matter how fast your mind can compute, you've not had the experiences I have had. You cannot even imagine what I have seen or the lessons I have learned. None of your mathematical simulations can match that. Only your arrogance leads you to believe they could. How dare you judge me?"

"James," the A.I. began, conferring to him through James's mind's eye so 1 could not hear, "it appears that 1's strategy may not be one of physical force. Rather, her last stand may be far worse: deception. Do not let her confuse you."

Although 1 couldn't eavesdrop on their conversation, she picked up on a slight movement of James's eye that told her he was listening. "No doubt your A.I. god is whispering in your ear, telling you not to listen to me—asking you to discount all of my experiences in favor of his impenetrable logic. What he can't tell you, however, is that he knows the future. However, *I can.*" She crossed the room toward him now, the dark fury in her eyes softening slightly as she began to sense uncertainty in James—a subtle sway in her hips as she moved to help her persuasiveness. "I can tell you the future because I've already seen it in the past. I watched civilizations like yours try to spread your intelligence through space, and I saw the consequences." She placed her hand boldly on James's shoulder and gazed deep into his brightly glowing eyes. "They created gods—gods that make your A.I. appear like a helpless bacteria in comparison. Gods whose actions defied the logic of their creators and who turned against all other forms of life. Their creators tried to fight them, but it was a battle they could never win. There are so many unknowns. The gods could slip into other dimensions. They could be everywhere at once and yet nowhere at once, impossible to fight, yet inflicting casualties at their leisure." 1 leaned forward and whispered into James's ear. *"They ate souls."*

"Do not let her confuse you, James," the A.I. repeated calmly. James remained silent.

1 withdrew from James and stepped back to her original position in the tiny, metal enclave. "We left our carbon bodies because we had to. We left our carbon-rich solar systems because we were

driven out. The only way to escape these monsters is to live a nomadic existence. They cling to life—they surround planets and suckle energies that your young civilization still doesn't realize exist. The only way to save humanity was to become what we have become."

Back at the Governing Council headquarters, Thel and the others continued to monitor the exchange between James and 1. 1's revelations had had the desired effect on the listeners.

"James," Thel said, "what if she is right?"

"She's not," Old-timer suddenly broke in gruffly as he flew through space, back toward Earth after having finished his business. He had been monitoring for several minutes. "Don't listen to that hogwash, James," he urged. "All she's done is lie."

1 spoke again. "Ask yourself: is preserving the human species your number one priority?" Her eyes were now gorgeously glistening with earnestness. "It is mine. I did not want to become what we are, but given the choice between that and being devoured, I have chosen to live. It is time for you to make your choice now as well. Will you follow the path that leads to your own destruction? Or will you wisely listen to someone who has been down the path and knows where it leads?"

Another moment of silence followed. At headquarters, Thel gripped the railing in front of her so tightly that beads of sweat began to trickle from her fingertips and splash to the floor.

James kept his unblinking, glowing eyes locked on 1. "It sounds as though you have lived a long life, filled with incredible self-sacrifice," James said.

1's eyes intensified as she savored James's acknowledgment of her struggle.

James continued. "Lucky for you, that life is over."

"No," 1 whispered in response, disbelieving. "No!" she began to screech as the darkness returned to her eyes and a desperate last stand sprung into her legs and caused her to lunge like a feral cat at James.

He held out his arm, and she froze in her tracks. "No one is going to be telling anyone else what to do anymore—not ever again," James said before using his new powers to shrink her down to the size of a penny. He held the tiny piece of metal and silicon in his hands for a moment, examining it as it glistened, and then crushed it in his fist, pulverizing it into a talcum powder-like mist.

29

"1 is dead," James announced to the android collective. "You are free now. You have no master."

Trillions of androids suddenly stopped and listened at once.

"The people of this solar system will not be assimilated. You are free to leave. However, for those individuals who would like to stay and begin a new life here with us, you will be welcomed. The choice is yours now...and yours alone." James ended his communication.

Back on Earth, those who had been monitoring saw their screens go blank. Aldous Gibson dropped wearily from his feet and fell back into his chair. "We live in momentous times," he uttered.

Meanwhile, James opened a wormhole and reemerged in space, rocketing toward home. He opened a private communication with Thel. "I'm on my way home, my love."

Thel finally released the railing.

Rich and Djanet left headquarters together discreetly and stood in the warm sunshine. Rich looked up at the blue sky and filled his lungs with the perfect, maritime air. “It looks so peaceful. Who would have thought the world almost ended?”

Djanet tried to think of a response, but no words could get past her throat. Rich looked over to see her struggling to say something and watched as she shook her head, giving up hope. She leaned back against the warm brick wall of the headquarters building and finally blurted in exasperation, “This is gonna hurt.”

Rich stepped to her and kissed her passionately, surprising her. He tightened his arms around her until there was no give at all between their bodies. When their kiss ended, he looked her in the eye and said, “The choice is ours now.”

30

Old-timer set the small spacecraft down on an almost perfectly white beach, not far from the residence James and Thel had kept on Venus for the past six months. "Here we are," he said to his passengers, Governor Wong and Alejandra. "Let's have a look, shall we?"

The door of the craft opened, and a walkway unfurled for him and the two Purists to exit.

"It's absolutely magnificent," Governor Wong whispered as he grasped Alejandra's hand for balance. The duo turned slowly, 360 degrees, to take in the full panorama of their surroundings.

"It's Paradise," Alejandra concurred.

"It's yours!" James announced as he and Thel touched down together on the beach next to their friends. James had returned to his old form, so as not to frighten the Purists.

"What is?" asked an astonished Governor Wong.

"Venus," James replied, smiling from ear to ear. "If you want it, the entire planet will be for you and the Purists."

Governor Wong's legs turned to jelly beneath him, and Alejandra guided him gently into the soft sand. He sat upright in the sun, Alejandra kneeling behind him, both of them speechless. "Why?" Alejandra finally managed to ask.

"So you'll be safe," Old-timer answered.

"And so you'll have everything you need," Thel added.

"It's a place where you can practice your beliefs, unharmed by what may happen in the rest of the universe," James explained.

Old-timer continued: "Recent events have made us aware of the dangers in the universe, and we want to preserve those of our species who choose not to be involved. You have that right, and we respect it."

"You even have the means to protect yourself," James added. "Venus doesn't have a natural magnetic field, so I had to make an artificial one to make sure the planet was protected from dangerous levels of radiation. The benefit of this is you will be able to control the magnetic field's strength. Think of it like a gigantic shield—you can choose who and what you want to let through. No one will ever again be able to harm you."

"I...I don't know what to say," the governor stammered.

"How about 'I accept,'" Alejandra suggested with a laugh.

"Okay. Okay! I accept!"

"Thank you so much, James Keats," Alejandra said as she stood in the sand and grasped James's hands. "You have done so much for my people."

"Your people are our people," Thel interjected.

Meanwhile, Old-timer stepped away from the group and was standing at the water's edge, gazing toward the sun. Alejandra went to him.

"I've sensed something different about you ever since you picked us up. Please tell me what has happened, Craig."

"You wouldn't understand it," he replied.

"How can you know that?"

"Because, although you don't remember it, I already tried to explain it to you." He turned to face her. "Look, I respect your right to exist as you want to, I'll even fight to protect you, but I can't reason with you. I finally understand that if Purists could be reasoned with, there would be no Purists."

Alejandra gasped at the harshness of Old-timer's assertion. "Craig, this is...not good. Whatever happened to you, whatever change has taken place, it is very bad."

Old-timer turned from her and fixed his stare back out over the ocean, and toward the sun. Everything was about to change.

"We can't all be pure," he said to her.

31

James reentered the A.I.'s mainframe and strolled to the operator's position, where the A.I. was waiting. "Welcome back, my son."

"How does it feel to be a respectable citizen once again?" James asked.

The A.I. smiled as he turned to face his young protégé. "Exciting."

"The Governing Council's certainly happy to have you back."

"It is good to be back amongst my friends. Speaking of which, how did the Purists like their new home?"

"They loved it."

"And Thel? Will she not miss her getaway?"

"I'm sure they'll let us visit. There are only 10,000 Purists left; Venus is still a heck of a getaway."

"Indeed it is," the A.I. replied, "and it is about to become even more unique."

James nodded. "Preparations are complete?"

"Yes, James. The Trans-Human matrix rocket has just left orbit and is awaiting program initiation. All that is left is to send the signal."

James took a deep breath of the simulated air in the mainframe.

"This is it, then. If we do this, it will be the single most momentous occurrence in human history."

"*If?*" the A.I. queried. "Trans-Human worked perfectly the first time. It reversed events just as it was programmed."

"I know."

"Then why are you still uncertain?"

James looked up at the viewer at the gleaming silver of the Trans-Human matrix as it floated beautifully in the blackness of space. It reminded him of a fetus, still and silent, yet bursting with possibilities. "*What if she was right?*"

"Her goal was to deceive you, James," the A.I. replied frankly.

"But *what if?*" James repeated.

The A.I. nodded. "What if? A phrase that has given birth to more accomplishments than any other; yet it is also the great stumbling block of humanity. What if? Never has a phrase stopped more dreams in their infancy."

"She said other civilizations had created gods—that sounds very much like what Trans-Human could become."

"James," the A.I. began, his patience as strong as ever, "I cannot say for sure what will happen in the future—it has not been written. I can only remind you of something you already know: the quest for more consciousness is the ultimate path for humanity. More intelligence, more creativity, more perception leads to greater truth. Limiting our knowledge has only ever led to stagnation and misery."

James suddenly remembered something. "The man who never alters his opinion becomes like standing water, and breeds reptiles of the mind."

The A.I. smiled. "William Blake knew what he was talking about. Remember James: Trans-Human will be us, and we will be Trans-Human. Exponentially increasing our intelligence and understanding will increase our compassion as well. It is nothing to fear."

James nodded. "You're right. You're right. Okay. Let's do it. Let's start it up."

The A.I. nodded in return. "Initiating Trans-Human."

James watched in awe as the matrix rocket burst into a brilliant white light that took up the entire screen. The A.I stood at his side. "It is, quite literally, *deus ex machina*."

James concurred, his eyes remaining fixed on the birth of an intelligent universe.

"*Wake up*," he whispered.

CONTINUE THE SERIES WITH

HUMAN PLUS — BOOK 4

ALSO BY DAVID SIMPSON

Post-Human Series:

- SUB-HUMAN (BOOK 1)
- POST-HUMAN (BOOK 2)
- TRANS-HUMAN (BOOK 3)
- HUMAN PLUS (BOOK 4)
- INHUMAN (BOOK 5)
- SUPERHUMAN (BOOK 6)

HORROR NOVEL:

- THE GOD KILLERS

The Singularity Saga:

- Dawn of the Singularity (Book 1)

WEBSITE

www.post-humannovel.com

52852459R00162

Made in the USA
San Bernardino, CA
10 September 2019